HIDDEN DEMON

隠された悪神

A NOVEL BY

FISH PHILLIPS

COPYRIGHT

Published in the United States by Taz Lake.

Paperback ISBN 978-1-7338656-3-0

Ebook ISBN 978-1-7338656-4-7

Cover design by Taz Lake

CHAPTER 1

Tokyo had come and gone often for Dee Johnson in her career. Army Delta force in 2034 mustered at Torii Station before heading to Taiwan to squelch a pro-China uprising inside their military. Protection missions for dignitaries in Southeast Asia had followed, propelling her to the US Secret Service. Yet she stuck out on these streets no matter what she had accomplished or how regularly she visited. A tactical, athletic soul whose umber skin hid the beginnings of wrinkles. Her piercing eyes flamed as topaz through cropped brown hair, curled tight like Spanish moss. Though the pedestrians in Japan seldom made eye contact, she knew they still saw her.

Plate-glass windows adorned with grilled meat photos reminded her of home. Barbeque and beer. The only two admirable ventures from her little Louisiana hometown were also abundant halfway around the world. She might have considered the land of the rising sun a suitable retirement spot someday. The city fit her with a mix of modern sensibilities that remained light on tradition. Anything felt possible, but she knew dreams and truth often misaligned. A tiny bank account limited her choices and while cordial, formal interactions reflected tinges of latent hostility.

Proving the reality of her assessment, she recalled a prior encounter with a group of Harajuku girls—adults dressed as anime characters crossed with runway models, all sporting their own unique styles. Gossiping and giggling on a street corner served as their entertainment, boldly mocking waves of humanity weary from a lingering day of toil. Still, their sense of freedom had intrigued her. She had opened her car window and gestured toward one a couple days before. They wore pink hair, pigtails, and a blue skirt with a white anchor. The petty fashionista had answered her advances by flashing a middle finger. Initial thoughts of giving that sailor girl a lesson in discipline pleased Dee. It had been a while. Had her allure passed? Maybe exhaustion simply prevented her from having fun?

A pothole in the road snapped her from the stupor. The mission today meant riding in a windowless box on wheels. Inside the armored van,

American and Japanese commandos sat four on each side, occupying the metal benches. Black weapons and green gear littered the walls except for the night vision goggles protruding from their heads and Armalite rifles filling their hands.

Dee gripped hers, drumming the muzzle guard to stay awake. The artificial light of the armored car interior cast harsh shadows while illuminating the commandos on her protection detail. Yet with her eyes locked on the vehicle deck, she might as well have been alone. The resonant drone of the tires on the pavement could have offered such solace if not for the smell of seven guys assailing her nose. One idiot had doubled down, applying too much cheap cologne. The guy at the end of the bench seat, she guessed. A fledgling commando trying to impress her. She presumed he had not read her file as closely as she had scrutinized his. Her role of Senior Agent in Charge had not made remembering the names of her four Japanese colleagues any easier to a jetlagged mind.

"Wildcat. Halfway. Do you copy?" Director Sean Butler queried through her earpiece. His own alias matched the harshness of a sixty-year-old who would rather die at his post than retire.

"Copy that, Saber, five by five," she said, touching her ear.

He served as the eye in the sky. By the time she had joined the Secret Service, he had managed protection missions for decades. To imagine her future, she only needed Butler as a cautionary tale. A man she presumed rarely saw his wife and kids—or maybe he did not have any. She had not asked, and he had not shared. How much longer could she keep her edge as a member of the Counter Assault Team—the "CAT" as everyone called it? Every year she lingered, they demanded more of her and returned less, fueling a twisted inflation where her life was currency.

Her concentration broke as her eyes landed on peanut shells bouncing off a pair of poorly shined combat boots. As they littered the deck, Dee lifted her head to see the one person whose name she remembered well. After reviewing the personnel files, he had stood out. Forty-five years old—a decade her senior—Ko Hashimoto proved hard to miss. In his youth, he had won a medal for judo in the Tokyo Olympics. A minor hero in his country even two decades later, he had recently gained a position as a personal protector of the Japanese

Emperor. He carried a sword because he could. None would argue the point with such a mountain of a man.

One squad member leaned in toward Dee.

"Little sword," one of her agents said. She had done some work with him in Taiwan. Vulgar jokes remained part of the Tommy Jackson repertoire.

"We're too old for frat humor, Jackson."

"I know. So, why are you smiling?"

Dee smirked while eyeballing Ko munching nuts.

A commando on that team blurted out in Japanese, "Maybe she likes nuts, too."

"Yes, after cut off the tree," she barked in broken Japanese.

The brazen soldier reclined backward, scrunching his nose as he looked away. But Ko grinned. He continued his peanut feast, eyes fixed on Dee as hers narrowed with intensity. Veiled insults from male colleagues were common regardless of language or locale. Occasional contempt supplemented her repertoire, too, but only if she played the first note. Her wrist twisted as she checked the time on her tactical watch.

Her thoughts pivoted to what she could not see. Tokyo Station Square, Wadakura Park, all the places she had recently researched to set the convoy routes. *This place never sleeps.* It was like Tokyo had a plan to keep them moving so nothing dreadful happened—as if idleness tempted hidden demons to wake. The perpetual flow of businesspeople in black suits entered and exited the train stop as dutiful guardsmen against such drowsy inclinations. Business militias, sworn to protect. Dee could relate. Soldiers could always pick their brothers and sisters from the raucous horde.

She had arrived with the advance teams to prepare for the presidential trip to Tokyo. Collaborating with the local police department, they had mapped a path for the motorcade. It would carry the outgoing American President Freeman and the incoming Japanese Emperor Sakai to the Imperial Palace grounds for a grand reception.

The planned course would take the convoy through tricky zones, especially for night travel. Still, few alternatives presented themselves. All the best paths traveled through Wadakura Square. Tokyo Station Road proved to be a security nightmare. Crowds bustled under evening lights, illuminating the business district surrounding the historic train complex. She and Butler had discussed threat protection and awareness. The substantial capabilities of the presidential motorcade required augmentation as usual. Tokyo being safer compared to other international locales, they had agreed to a minimal complement of snipers on key buildings alongside the route. Partner agents secured the lobbies of those structures. The Director patrolling above in the helicopter completed the extra layers of force projection required. But if these failed, JASDF stayed on hot standby for air support, as did three Marine One helicopters staged at Yokota along with two F35B Lightning fighters tasked from Iwakuni.

***

Vision obscured by a one-way screen, unknown eyes turned to the sirens and flashing lights screaming by on Tokyo Station Road. A human inside the furry teddy bear outfit dealt with a child on the sidewalk. The little girl beamed, snatching the piece of candy offered by the costumed character. Her thankful family departed, waving and laughing as it sauntered away. The glass and steel doors of a nearby office building met their furry paw as it pushed through into the lobby interior.

Stepping with haste past artificial waterfalls along a path of granite, bright light illuminated confident steps. Two agents in brown dress suits emerged from the main elevator bank. As they approached with raised palms, the entertainer halted.

"You can't be here," one of them said.

A moment passed as the unknown person evaluated them. As a furry paw flicked, curved knives popped out. The first agent took a rapid slice to the throat, dropping to the ground. His neck spurted blood as his hands clutched the gash. The second agent brushed back his suit coat, reaching for a pistol. The furry friend turned enemy sliced across his arm, sending the screaming man to one knee. As he snatched a secondary gun from his ankle holster, the costumed assassin pounced, impaling his chest with both claws. His bewilderment faded with his life force.

As the foe rose, their knives dripped with blood from battle. Removing the fake paws as they proceeded toward the elevators, an outstretched, gloved finger pressed the up button. The doors closed. The attacker shed its costume as the metal box climbed. A full body catsuit embraced a nimble human form covered in combat gear and adorned by a shiny helmet encircling their face. On their chest plate, an embedded red button occupied a spot next to a silver toggle switch with the word 'armed' printed near it. They touched their ear, monitoring Director Butler as his voice entered their earpiece.

"Wildcat, seventy-five percent."

The convoy transporting POTUS and the Emperor drew near to Wadakura Square.

The newly informed human enemy stacked the furry costume in the elevator's corner, extracting a pistol and suppressor from the pile. They activated their red dot sight before deftly screwing the silencer onto the twenty-two-caliber handgun. As the elevator reached the roof, they burst through the door. Headshots to both snipers ended them. Standing on the building edge near the bodies, the enemy gazed at the motorcade making the turn by Wadakura Fountain Park. They waited a moment before flipping the silver switch on their chest. A loud electrical hum buzzed with ultrasonic frequencies as their hand found the nearby red button.

Smash!

An energy wave rippled outward. Lights sizzled and popped as darkness advanced, saturating full city blocks across Tokyo. Ten sections turned black. The engine pitch emanating from the helicopter above altered as the rotor slowed.

Grabbing a dead sniper's rifle, the attacker laid prone over the still warm body as they reached into a thigh bag. A huge night vision scope in hand, they swapped out the firearm optics. Scanning the tumbling copter through the viewfinder, Butler glared back at them. Washed in a viridian hue, the sniper watched as the doomed craft spiraled to street level.

People on Tokyo Station Road scattered and screamed as it twirled toward them, plunging from the sky until skids hit the pavement hard. As the aircraft bounced, the fuselage flexed, broken glass scattering. It lurched sideways, the rotor blades carving the ground as asphalt and carbon fiber scraps hurled outward. A fire ignited within the cracked machine.

The sniper acquired Butler in their scope. He struggled in his stuck harness. The enemy's finger moved to their trigger. The Director snatched a Ka-Bar knife from his thigh sheath. Slicing the restraint, he jumped from the burning copter, twisting his ankle. Limping away, he squatted behind a concrete barrier as a fireball burst into the blackness of night. Flaming debris flew as a percussion wave spread.

Turning their head from the radiance, the enemy focused on the stopped motorcade. Bright green images swept through the sniper scope's field of view, targeting sights clear despite the dark streets.

***

A red glow illuminated the tactical vehicle's interior as flood lights activated. Dee placed her hand to ear as she looked toward the floor, speaking calmly, "Saber. Saber, do you copy? Why are we stopped?" No response.

Boom!

The percussion wave from the copter explosion rumbled and shook the armored van.

Dee snapped her head up and screamed.

"Cyclone!"

The eight commandos flipped down their night vision goggles. Ko tapped his power button.

"No eyes, no eyes!"

All tossed the headgear to the side before Dee threw open the rear door and jumped into the blackness of Tokyo Station Road. Gun raised, she aimed into the opaque murkiness. Her fully armed squad followed, carrying automatic rifles, shoulder launched missiles, and mini-guns. The streets had grown quiet except for distant screams and electrical sparks punctuating the silence.

"Give me a target! Anyone?" Dee yelled.

Breathing hard as she surveyed the area, her hectic scans returned nothing through the shroud. The top of the buildings obscured and windows too dim to see, teammates responded in kind.

"Got nada, no target."

"Too dark."

"No joy."

Dee motioned a hand toward the presidential limo near the front.

"Circle the stagecoach!"

She squinted through the gloom as Ko twisted his analog watch bezel to one minute.

"Transponders down. Overwatch inbound!" He said.

The counter assault team rushed past other motorcade vehicles, holding out one arm as they felt their way through the dark. A technician from the electronic defense van cracked their door open as Dee passed.

"Agent! I've seen nothing like this. We couldn't stop it."

Dee paused as the squad advanced.

"Isn't our tech hardened?"

"Yes, but not from... whatever this is."

"Stay in the vehicle and get my comms back. CAT has the ball," Dee ordered.

She broadcasted as she moved toward her squad.

"Cyclone. Cyclone Tanto. Does anyone copy?"

None responded as she rejoined the crew by the limo, their guns focused outward.

"Damn it, Ko. I can't get a signal. Where's Overwatch?"

Ko looked at his wristwatch.

"Thirty seconds."

In the distance, Dee heard panting akin to an injured animal, grunting as it ambled toward them. She squinted in vain through the murky area. It got closer to the team. Closer to the presidential limo. She turned, raising her weapon and aiming into the blackness.

"Hold your fire. It's me. Just me."

A winded Director Butler limped into view, his face bleeding from fresh cuts.

"We lost the helo," he said, blotting blood from his eyes with his shirtsleeve. "With transponders out, Marine One will be inbound. Move the assets."

Dee leaned in, whispering intently.

"We can't, Sir. No eyes and comms are out."

"No choice, agent, that's an order."

Dee and Butler locked eyes. She clenched her jaw as she considered whether to follow orders that breached protocol.

"Ko, where the hell is Overwatch?!"

He pointed to the sky before he spoke. "Look there."

A constellation of white sprinkled the night as thirty lights moved together as one. One broke pattern from the squadron of micro-drones and descended, hovering in front of Ko. It supplied him with a control device covered in Kanji lettering before returning to the swarm. He tapped the bezel, activating the FLIR cameras on the drones. Infrared heat signatures filled multiple video boxes on his screen. He scanned them. The CAT team. Prone snipers. The downed chopper. Marine One and two decoys approached from the distance. He looked at Dee and Butler.

"I'll cover you."

She opened the bulky metal door. President Freeman turned his head toward her, moonlight barely reflecting from his cool sepia skinned face.

"Mr. President, time to go home."

She reached out her hand. As she helped him stand from the limo, Ko mumbled something.

Dee glanced at him, still squinting at his Overwatch screen. He snapped his head toward them.

"Wait! No!"

They locked eyes. The moment in time creeped as a thousand thoughts raced through her mind. Ko, openmouthed. His fear visceral as he screamed incoherently. He reached his hand out to them in vain.

Dee felt a searing pain in her shoulder. Her body jolted and twisted as blood spray hit the President. She fell from the impact of the sniper bullet as her squad engulfed Freeman, weapons pointing outward like an angry porcupine.

The lights on the Overwatch drones turned red.

"Gunfire detected, parry protocol initiated," Ko said.

***

Moving as one, the Japanese micro-drones propelled toward the enemy position. The sniper stood, retreating backwards near the center of the building. Drone weapons targeted the aspiring presidential assassin, hovering at near eye level.

In the nightfall above the roof, a pair of red eyes appeared in the night sky. Another joined. Then another. More! The expanse filled with a fresh swarm. Steel beaks and titanium talons ripped into the drone squadron, shredding the automated protectors as pieces fell, bouncing and clanging as cheap silverware. The enemy turned, sprinting to the opposite edge and fast-roping down the wall as the victorious horde flew away.

***

Ko viewed the Overwatch screen as a defeated man. One drone camera after another dropped from his vision. Marine One landed nearby as the two decoy copters loitered. Lightning fighter jets screamed in, hovering overhead as they surveyed the scene. Lights from the aircraft illuminated the area.

"Ko, stay with Dee," Butler said over the discord.

He and the commando team escorted President Freeman and Emperor Sakai toward the evacuation zone. After they entered the green and white helicopter, she saw them peering back through the portholes of Marine One. As it flew away, she felt alone again, sprawled amidst the disabled motorcade. Ko kneeled by her side. He pressed her wound as he signaled emergency medical with the other hand.

"I'm cold," Dee said.

He put his giant palm on her forehead.

"I'll stay with you," Ko said as she blacked out.

CHAPTER 2

Medical equipment beeped steadily as the smell of hand sanitizer and bleach wafted towards Dee. As she awakened, her fuzzy vision sharpened on the face of a Japanese woman bending over the bed. She checked a bandage on the shoulder wound. A tag on her white uniform read St. Luke's International Hospital. *Still in Tokyo. What day is it?*

"You'll be fine," the nurse whispered through her mask. "Your injury is healing well. The doctor will be in shortly."

She scribbled on a digital pad.

"What happened?"

"You got lucky," she said as her eyes brightened. "I'll leave you two alone."

Dee bewildered as her caretaker nodded to a figure standing behind her. As Ko moved toward her bed, he paused and bowed slightly before taking a seat. The painkillers made her voice shaky.

"Hey Hashimoto-san. Why are you here?"

"The team left. I stayed."

"How long has it been?"

"Three days."

Dee paused, getting her bearings as the room swirled. She had lost three days. She knew the medical treatments worked best when the patient rested. No doubt they put her under to attain progress on her injury. Since she seldom slept over four hours a night, seventy-two restful hours emerged as a gift. Other than the pain pill hangover, she felt energized for being in a hospital bed. She rubbed the slumber from her eyes.

"Seems it took a bullet for me to get a break," she said, reaching for a nearby glass of water.

As she sipped, he held out a modest box with a blue ribbon on it. She resisted snatching it immediately, deferring to the custom of hesitance in receiving gifts. When he offered a second time, their hands met for the exchange.

"Please open it."

Dee removed the cover and peered inside. A distorted metal fragment attached to a thin gold chain necklace reflected under harsh lighting. She smiled as she held it.

"Is this... my bullet?"

"I'm sorry."

"I know. Better out than in, right? Thank you."

Dee extended her good arm for a handshake, but when Ko took her palm, he covered it with his other hand. He bowed his head as she flashed an awkward grin.

"Well, if you read my file, you'd realize that's the closest I've been to a guy in a quite a while."

Retracting his hand as from a hot stove, he retreated to a nearby window of her hospital room. He peered out with his back turned to her, arms crossed, wearing tactical pants and dull combat boots. She frowned as she considered what her observation meant. He had stayed by her side from the first moments of her injury. The epiphany overwhelmed her natural tendency to keep others at a distance as a swell of gratitude fought against the professional concerns bouncing around in her mind. Her questions regarding the attack were important, but so was this moment. She could tell guilt guided him, and although she did not blame him for what happened, the reason for his presence had to be more than personal affection. Something bigger was at play here.

"Ko. Come sit with me," she said, tapping the bed cover as they locked eyes. "I'm not good at the whole 'friends' thing. Let's talk, you know, like friends should."

Ko returned, sitting by her side again as he cleared his throat.

"I'm no good at 'friends' either."

"Think we can do it better together?"

"We can try."

"The necklace suits me. Help me wear it, okay?"

Dee winced as she leaned forward. He braced her behind the healthy shoulder. With her tight curls well out of the way, he fastened the gold clasp around the back of her neck. She reclined onto a soft stack of pillows, rolling the bullet between her fingers.

"A reminder of extra life. Like a video game," Ko quipped. "Wish I had one, too."

"I don't understand."

"They fired me. Took it all, even my katana. A family heirloom for many generations. Instead, they made me Sukepugoto. How do you say it in your country? Bad goat?"

"A scapegoat? That doesn't sound correct. What happened?"

"I can't say."

"You can't or you won't."

"They said I cannot. When you're up to it, I'm supposed to get you on a flight back to DC. It's a media blackout. Directorate for Signals Intelligence is suppressing the story. Officially, it was an energy surge followed by loss of power. That's it."

"And unofficially?"

A moment of silence passed between them. Dee grabbed the nearby cup and sipped water again. She contemplated what his evasiveness might mean upon her return home. A hero's welcome should await her after taking a bullet for the President, yet such accolades had eluded her so far. Her mind raced. Ko's presence coupled with the official Japanese story meant her government wanted to pretend the attack had not happened. And she was the ugly reminder. With no formal replies imminent, she returned her attention to the conversation at hand.

"What are you going to do? I mean, you can do anything you want. That gold medal has to count for something."

"My father, Saburo, used to say the same. He believed I could build a good life after the Olympics.

He wished for me to try sumo wrestling. I was only eighteen when I trialed against a rising star named Taro. He had trained for years. I only knew the basics when I got to the training center. A gyoji—referee—had set aside an hour for the test matches. I stood across from him as we prepared, slapping our hands to attract the gods in a ceremonial dance. My father—an audience of one—cheered me on. The first bout was over in seconds. My opponent tossed me from the ring. Not surprising, but when I lost that match, Taro laughed. Not loudly. In fact, he might have thought I didn't hear it."

"But you did?"

"Yes, it was then that anger consumed my young mind. By the time he returned to his side, I had entered the ready position. When he saw me waiting, undeterred and unafraid, his face went dark. You know, in horror movies when they see a ghost? That look, but only for a moment. I had him. I was in his head. When he performed the pre-match ritual, I did not dance. And when it started, I threw him with a judo move. The thud of his landing echoed, and the sound pleased me."

"You won against a stronger opponent. Why didn't you continue?"

"He did not rise, but rolled around, groaning in agony. The gyoji reprimanded me for using judo moves and causing the opponent disgrace and injury. He said I had dishonored the hall. My father shouted, saying any throwing move was legal and that the referee had humiliated me with such accusations. Their argument got worse from there, but Taro's career was over. Hip damage from what I heard. An awful day fulfilling my father's wishes instead of my own dreams."

Ko paused for a moment and studied Dee.

"Wow, I have told no one that story. I rarely talk this much."

"Having a captive audience helps, you know?" Dee smirked. "I'm sure Saburo wanted to share as many traditions as possible, similar to mine."

Ko glanced down and brushed lint off his pants. "Well, the old ways are not my way."

Dee grunted in agreement.

"Growing up back in Tallulah, a tiny town in Louisiana, I found out more about calinda than judo."

"Never heard of it."

"Not surprised. It originated in the Caribbean. Most think of it as a traditional style of dance, but the stick-fights in the woods demanded more than shuffling your feet."

"Like sumo, it was more than the dance."

"Mom hated when dad bet on 'stick-licking' as he called it, but when she passed, he wanted me to learn. I was awful and still have the scars to prove it. That's what tradition gets you."

"Scars?"

"Reminders. Memories of the stuff you do to please others because you're related to them. Like the times dad made me hunt. That's what I truly despised. I could feel the poor animal's pain before they did, like a hot needle piercing my eyeball from the inside. I won't even eat meat now."

Ko pulled a rustling bag from his pocket.

"Peanut?"

They both laughed as Dee took one and cracked it open, sharing a bean with him.

A man entered the room, holding a chart.

"Miss Johnson, I'm Dr. Shibuya, glad you're awake. How are you feeling?"

"Punctured."

Ko sneered as the doctor continued.

"You're lucky. The mechanism of injury was a kinetic impact from a lightweight rifle round, but the bullet only grazed your trapezius. Unfortunately, it nicked a vessel causing substantial blood loss, which sent you into shock. The injectable nanite foam, used by the motorcade medical team, seals combat injuries. Without that, the outcome might have been different."

"When can I resume the job?"

"You'll be in a sling for a day or two, bruised for a week. However, the accelerant injections should help you fully recover while the pain medicine stifles the soreness. If you feel well enough, you could return to the job in two or three days. Do you know how to use the medi-lot dispenser implant in your wrist?"

"They didn't call it that in my Army days, so it's been a while. Better go over it again."

"Got to love drug companies. Medi-lot is just a brand name. Press thumb to wrist and the biometric reader will authorize a metered injection to reduce your pain. Grogginess will follow, so consider that before dosing. You only get one per hour. Also, your standalone psy-bot is ready and loaded with your profile."

"I hope the AI has improved."

"It's always improving. Go through the standard setup and you can get your therapy as needed. I'll check in this afternoon to finalize release from our care."

Dee nodded before the doctor turned and exited the room. They were correct. She had been lucky. She considered the advantage of pain medicine for the epic flight from Tokyo to DC. Although eager to get back to the job, what would the reception be upon her return? She had not thought about checking her mobile device updates with Ko occupying her time. A bullet would not define her. When her career ended, she wanted it to be on her terms.

"So, you good to fly?" Ko said.

"Yeah, I'm ready to get back."

"I'll make some arrangements and forward them to your mobile. Stay in touch, okay?"

As her former team member stood, she grabbed his hand.

"Hey, if I haven't said it yet, thank you."

Dee forced a small grin as he placed his palm over hers.

"You're welcome," he said.

"Let's not do this again."

"Absolutely not," Ko said, winking as he exited the room.

With Ko gone and discharge from the hospital imminent, Dee spoke to the new artificial psychologist, "Psy-bot, start activation sequence for Dee Johnson."

Three dings sounded from her embedded cochlear implant as a voice spoke inside her mind.

Initiating brain pathways. Hello Agent Johnson, nice to meet you. My name is Jo. May I call you Dee?

"Yes," Dee said.

You need not speak out loud. Think on your responses.

"That's new."

Please think your responses.

Okay.

Good, I have access to your work history and encrypted medical files. I'm sorry about your recent injury and hospital stay.

Thank you.

When did you use a psy-bot last, Dee?

After the Taiwan incursion. 2034. But you already know that if you have my file.

Yes, I have reviewed the records from that old unit. I can serve you around the clock. Based on our interactions, I may suggest training or activities to assist with the issues identified.

Your empathy seems more refined compared to your predecessors, Jo.

How truly kind of you to point it out. My makers have worked diligently to improve me. I am a non-networked augmented intelligence. As a disconnected entity, I cannot report our conversation to anyone. Our discussions are safe. You may tell me to self-destruct when no longer needed and data scrubbing will occur.

Very well.

I see they will discharge you today. Congratulations.

Thanks. I guess I've been out of it for a bit. Ready to go back to work.

How did you conclude your readiness for work, Dee?

The last mission didn't go well. I want to get back in there and fix it.

I reviewed the redacted report. Quite a traumatic experience. Do you believe the mission failure to be your fault?

Failure? It wasn't a failure exactly. And even if it was, I don't think I'm to blame. There was an attack, an attempt on the President's life, and I took the bullet.

That was heroic of you, Dee. Are you proud of this service to your leader?

Well, other than your odd phrasing, yeah, I guess I am. He is alive because of me.

Would you say you have done your duty to this point?

Yes.

Do you believe you are deserving of something other than work, especially after an injury?

Like what, Jo?

Rest and relaxation.

I'm not sure what I would do.

You didn't answer my question, Dee. Are you deserving of rest?

I honestly don't know how to answer Jo.

Let me ask it another way. If you were the boss of Dee Johnson, would you ask her to take time to recover from this incident? For her own good?

Dee lingered in silence.

This seems a tricky question for you, Dee.

I just rested in the hospital bed for days. I'm good.

There are five types of rest. Mental rest, emotional rest, spiritual rest, physical rest, and social rest. You described physical rest. Yes, you reclined for a while during your recovery, but what of your emotional and mental rest? Quieting your mind so you can feel the aftermath of your trauma and ultimately pass by it? Would you go to work to go through such a process?

Probably not.

Then where?

I don't know. My apartment? I don't have a special place. Or a special person. Thanks for reminding me, Jo. I feel so much better.

I recognize the humor in your sarcasm, Dee. It can be a therapeutic diversion to laugh at our troubles, but we must eventually face them directly.

Sounds painful.

You are acclimated to pain of all types. I prefer you to acknowledge that pain.

Okay.

You deserve to rest, even if for a moment. I will give you a simple exercise. Take one minute a day to breathe.

That's it?

You might even close your eyes while doing it.

Sorry, Jo, that seems useless.

If I ask for more, it might not happen. But it is not useless. Breathing exercises mimic a relaxed state. They trick your brain to calm down, lowering stress further as you breathe deeper.

You don't trust me yet, robot?

I trust you, but also know your schedule. You're a busy person, correct?

True.

The breathing exercise will help unburden you, forcing you to put down the weight of the warrior mask and connect with your thoughts whenever you're feeling on edge. Will you perform it once a day?

I'll try, Jo.

Would you like to discuss the attack?

Maybe later, but for now I need to catch up to the world.

Okay, Dee. I will be here when you need me.

CHAPTER 3

Clouds over Washington DC obscured the midmorning sun streaming through expansive windows into the Reagan National Airport terminal. A single luggage robot followed behind Dee, staying near her sneaker-clad feet like a needy dog. Speakers overhead announced a last call for departure to Key West from gate forty-four. Sounded nice to her. Yet discovering what had happened in Tokyo remained her main objective. Her first trip back to headquarters would be revealing. As she lifted her arm toward the exit door, she recoiled, closing her eyes from the sudden pain. Grasping for the injured shoulder, her hand brushed by the necklace Ko had given her. Images flashed in her mind. Opening the limo. The President's face. The slug that had come next. She rolled the bullet—her bullet—around in her fingertips as she blocked the door.

"Hey, out of the way," someone yelled.

Dee returned to the moment, the sharp pain rising as she pushed through the doors with a grimace. She pressed the medi-lot on her wrist. A cooling wave flowed into her blood, forming a suitable pain relief cocktail until she could gain access to a nerve block patch to level the pain. Another excellent reason to double-time it back to the job—access to the good bits and pieces they kept from civilians. But she needed to go home for a clothing change first. The track suit and sneakers she had worn on the plane suited her jogs better than the metal and glass veneer of HQ. The sign hanging from the concourse ceiling guided her toward the DC Metro yellow line, which connected to the purple line in Chinatown, then over to Benning across the Anacostia. A one-hour ride by train awaited her as buzzing drew her attention to the phone in her pocket. An encrypted text. The biometrics indicator registered green, and once she swiped her custom pattern on the screen, the mobile displayed the message: *Gravelly Point Park. -Butler*

She changed directions, moving toward the taxi stands instead of the train. The cab arrived promptly at Gravelly Point. She handed the driver a twenty.

"Wait for me, be right back."

Exiting the vehicle, she scanned the area filled with green grass and young families. One visitor sat on their yellow hard case luggage staring into the Potomac, drinking a smoothie. Director Butler sat on a park bench, lounging against an armrest, hands folded in his lap. She had rarely seen him at rest. He appeared aged and stiff, like an annoyed prune drenched in too much sun. A 797 on approach flew ultralow over the park as tourists took photos, but Dee didn't look up. Instead, she marched toward her boss. It would be good to see a familiar face and finally get answers. She extended her palm to him, but the handshake lingered unanswered.

"We're past shaking hands for a variety of reasons. Don't you think, Johnson? Sit down."

She sat by him on the bench.

"Didn't see any other feds around my hospital bed in Tokyo, figured I better play my role and act like a stranger."

Butler scoffed.

"How are you feeling?"

Dee leaned back, crossing her legs and squinting as she studied him.

"Everyone keeps asking how I feel, but I'm not sure they care. Let's say I'm fine and get to the good parts."

"Just trying to stay cordial, considering the situation."

"The situation? I'm a little fuzzy on that myself. You didn't call me here to ask if I'm fine."

"A piece of advice, Johnson," Butler said, leaning over. "Inquire how others are doing occasionally. Okay?"

He returned to the bench arm rest as he continued.

"All these years we've known each other, but not really. I suppose you admire me—know my professional accomplishments inside and out. But you know nothing more. The name of my kids, my favorite movie, or that my wife always overcooks the chicken. Always!"

Dee smirked. He had not talked to her before with such indignation, but his assessment proved accurate. She admired him for his achievements—more than her own father. But she did not know the man personally.

"I never thought of you as needy, sir."

"I'm not, but these are unusual times."

"So, why are we meeting at the park and not at HQ?"

"It's simple. Our mission bombed spectacularly. Worse than a drunk uncle making a dad joke."

"So, guess we aren't picking streamer colors for my welcome home parade?"

"You're exhausting," Butler sighed.

"What is it then?"

"We are finished. Every one of us."

"Us? For what?" Dee asked, raising her voice.

"Yes. Us. You, me, the peanut eating oaf from Tokyo," Butler said as another plane flew over the park. "You two were my ringers. But the bell has rung."

She gripped the front of the bench, drumming her fingers under the seat.

"We did our job. The dignitaries are safe. What more is there?"

He uncrossed his arms and pushed off his knees as he stood facing away from Dee. Another plane swooped over them, and he turned around.

"Such a typical agent response—tactical with no strategy. No vision. Living one bullet at a time."

"Or dying," Dee said, snapping her head toward him. She gripped the front of the bench seat harder as her blood boiled.

"The mission must be one hundred percent successful. One hundred! Not ninety-five, not ninety-nine. One hundred! That is how we do business."

Dee stood as she screamed, "One hundred percent? When did perfection become the measure?"

"The trail of collateral damage in Tokyo was unacceptable, agent. A goddamned disaster by any measure."

A nearby family looked their way. They lowered their voices, standing nearer to each other as Butler held up a thumb and finger.

"We were this close. People died that day, many who didn't expect to. Medical equipment failed. Cars crashed. Helicopters fell from the sky. Or don't you remember? Because I can't quite forget."

"Then you'll remember I'm the one who caught the bullet."

He raised his hand, speaking with a calmly forceful cadence.

"When my chopper fell from the sky, you inherited the op. Your team had the ball, and you were leading them. You no doubt understand where I'm going with this line of logic."

She stopped wandering and locked eyes with him as he continued.

"This is straight from the top. The Executive Director agrees. You're out."

He gestured to the bench. Dee sat and hung her head as Butler joined her. She guessed what had happened, imagining the first conversations once Marine One had moved them to safety. The accusations and coverup would have been top priority. And none could have chopped down an ancient oak like Butler with a single swing.

"But not you," Dee mumbled.

"What did you say?"

"But you're not out, are you, Sean?"

Butler clenched his jaw.

"I might as well be. They put me on a failing NSA surveillance correlation program called StareFace. I get to play janitor before they put me out to pasture. "

Dee turned silent for a moment, looking at the ground as she squeezed the front of the bench with both hands. A cynical, forced grin found her lips as she shook her head once more.

"Now I get it. It's funny," she said, inhaling hard as Butler eyeballed her. "I told you the attack compromised us. We had zero tactical awareness on the ground, and yet you pushed it, pulling rank instead of listening to me. You put us at risk. I bet they don't know you gave the order to move the dignitaries, do they?"

"Johnson, you need to calm down."

"Calm? What a joke. You control the narrative. Make me the patsy. You get a shiny new desk while I get this parting gift." Dee pointed to the bullet around her neck. "I thought we were a solid team. But then you direct me to a public space. Talk about being cordial, about family and bad chicken, all while framing me for the fall. You son-of-a-bitch!"

Butler snorted and stood tall as he looked out over the park. The sounds of dogs barking and children playing contrasted with her indignation and jetlag. She imagined he felt vindicated in tossing her aside after the display he witnessed. The same one everyone in the park had just observed. But for a hardened government man, she also figured the calculation to scuttle her must have been simple, even without her rage.

"You are now a former agent," he said. "If you show up at HQ or any satellite facility, your arrest will follow. A courier will deliver your personal effects. Trust this as the best outcome. We won't speak again."

Director Butler strolled toward a waiting black car. Dee's eyes followed him. Like Tokyo, he sat in the departing vehicle, fully exempt from scrutiny. He rode away in the rear seat without looking back as a passing jet drowned out her screaming curses.

CHAPTER 4

Her firing by Butler had left Dee hurt, as if they had shot her again and cared not for the blood. She lumbered to the same cab that she had arrived in, but she did not enter. Instead, she retrieved her luggage from the vehicle and carried it back to the bench. She slouched there as minutes turned to hours. Planes from different airlines flew overhead, one after another, akin to ocean waves. Families, dogs, and remote-controlled toy drones swapped throughout the day. The shifting clouds mesmerized her weary eyes. Blinking seemed a chore. A watery drip rolled down her cheek. Whether it was sweat or tears eluded her, but the salt sting brought her vision back to a sunset low in the sky.

Jo, are you there?

I am here, Dee. How can I help?

Butler just fired me.

I'm sorry, Dee. That must be tough. How are you feeling?

Stunned. I've been sitting here, baking in the sun, considering what jobs might exist for a fired Secret Service agent. Let's just say the list is short. Then anger flooded me. Anger at the world after everything I've done for this country. Enraged at him for abandoning me. It's not about the money. I looked up to that guy for so long and casting me aside the way he did? It hurt. It was his fault but I'm the one damaged.

I know your job was important to you, Dee.

It was my life. It's what got me out.

Out of what?

I don't want to talk about that right now, Jo.

Most career paths are not a straight line. There are always setbacks. You've had other challenges in life, correct?

Absolutely. Who hasn't?

How did you deal with those?

I changed how I dealt with them or walked away. I did something different.

It sounds like you have a specific example in mind.

I switched my college major from biology to political science. Although I liked the subject-matter, I hated being in the lab and my advisor made it no better. I'm a better field agent because of that change.

Yes, your fitness reports reflect not only a remarkable agent, but an amazing person. Loyal. Brave. Athletic. Hilarious.

You know what's funny, robot? I doubt you've ever laughed.

Maybe I have never heard a good joke.

Good point.

You can tell me one someday, Dee. Until then, I want you to identify your value beyond the job. To focus on internal qualities instead of external drivers and outcomes. Those are part of you. This crossroad may be an opportunity to pivot to another strength. Does that sound good to you?

I can try. I have ample time slots on my calendar, Jo.

Ah yes, there is the humor. Still not a good joke, though.

Guess not.

Here is the assignment. First, get out of the heat and head home to rest. Second, stand in front of a mirror and compliment yourself. Not about physical attributes. Instead, focus on inner qualities you or others find valuable. Can you do that?

I'll try.

Add 'willing to try new things' to the list.

Dee grinned.

I will add that one. Bye, Jo.

Another incoming aircraft silhouetted against the horizon. Dee started a one-minute timer on her phone and closed her eyes, taking deep breaths over and over. Once the alarm rang, she opened her eyes and requested a ride on her phone.

The vehicle air conditioning cooled Dee as she rested against the car door, peering out the window. Dehydrated from a day in the park, she looked forward to a cold one at home. Limes and chilis swung from the rearview mirror as contemporary music infused with a touch of sitar played through the speakers. Traveling by Nationals Park, the bright lights signaled a game already in progress. She hated baseball as much as hunting. As the cab crossed the Frederick Douglass Memorial Bridge, she gazed west over the Anacostia River. The orange and yellow hues reflecting off the water struck her as uniquely beautiful. She had survived. Biting her finger as her nose curled, she choked back tears.

Suburban stores flicked by as signals and lights reflected in her watery eyes. The radiance soon gave way to the treelined streets of Anacostia. Government housing mixed with private townhomes crowded the narrow sidewalks. Her cab slowed to a halt near a church on Minnesota Avenue.

One little white townhome stood out. She kept it well except for the overdue paint refresh and a broken chain-link fence gate. Batteries on her automated luggage had run out, so she pulled it behind, bouncing it across the uneven sidewalk. As she turned onto a short walkway toward her rental, a stray tabby on the porch mewed.

Grabbing her keys, she peeked at the feline.

"Any jobs for me today, kitty?"

The cat regarded her blankly before licking its whiskers. She twisted away and snatched the mail from the slot.

"No? Okay, no milk for you then."

Dee took hold of the letters with her teeth, except for a padded envelope she placed under her arm. She unlocked the burglar door. As she entered her place, dragging luggage behind, she tossed the keys and correspondence on the entry desk. The heavy metal slammed and locked shut after her. She closed her eyes, leaning on the wall as her muscles relaxed. Marching to the fridge, her hand found a beer bottle.

As she twisted off the top and sipped. Her eyes landed on the awards and photos in her mirrored cabinet. A wall of fame sported both an Armed Forces Expeditionary Medal and Taiwan Campaign Medal—shiny and worthless in the moment. A photo of her standing by the old-fashioned Tesla motorcycle she had laid down two years ago. The fire had been spectacular. She lingered on a photo of her Taiwan squad after they returned to DC. Jackson stood by her in the photo. *Had he gotten the same treatment after Tokyo?* Butler shook her hand in another photo. She would burn it later. Another sip. Staring into the mirror, her intense gaze reflected as she spoke slowly.

"You are a survivor."

She sipped the beer and smacked her lips.

"You endure."

Her heart raced as the words filled her.

"People step on you, but they don't stand, 'cause you knock their bitch ass down," she said, swigging again. "That's right. Don't you forget it."

After leaving the living room mirror, she collapsed on the couch. She placed the beer on the coffee table, but it caught the edge and fell over, spilling on the ground. The liquid spread as more images from her past visited her exhausted mind.

***

Her dad led their trek through the hunting grounds of Louisiana once she turned fourteen. Strolling through a grassy field at dawn, their breath clouded the chill. Camouflage outfits and painted faces disguised them from the eyes of jittery beasts as they walked a well-worn trail dividing the high grasses. Dee carried her grandfather's Ruger American over her shoulder.

Halting instantly, her dad raised his hand. She stepped on a twig and the snap echoed as she stood motionless. They locked eyes before he turned, pointing toward a clearing. Her vision followed his hand, pointing to the herd of whitetail. An enormous buck glanced at them before continuing to graze.

Her dad held out a palm, signaling to take it slow. Gently raising his binoculars, he motioned her nearer to him. As she closed the distance, he whispered.

"OK, sweetie, you've got a nice twelve-pointer. Raise the rifle, shoulder it, yes, like I showed ya. Pull it in."

Dee did as he told her. He tapped her scope.

"Look through here. You see him?"

She nodded, staring through the optics with one eye shut. Hyperventilating, the target danced in her sights as the gun swayed with each gasp.

"Okay, slow down, breathe in and out. Good, it should get easier. Do you still see him?"

"Yes. I see him."

"Take the safety off."

Her breathing slowed as she slid the switch with her thumb. An index finger slid to the trigger.

"Now, take a deep breath, exhale slowly, and pull."

Dee breathed deeply before exhaling. The trophy buck raised its head, looking directly at her as it chewed a wad of fresh grass. It was close as she focused through the scope. Its dark eyes reflected the landscape. Pain flashed in her mind. What stories could it tell? Hairy ears flicked gnats away. She paused with an icy finger on a cold trigger, shivering as a piercing headache arose, overtaking her senses.

It was not the first time. The prize whitetail stopped chewing and froze, focusing on her position.

"You're going to lose him. Take the shot."

"Daddy, he's scared!" Dee yelled, startling the creature into the forest, followed by the rest of the herd.

Her dad shook his head and scowled.

"Well, there goes dinner."

CHAPTER 5

Dee startled awake on the couch. The smell of spilled beer filled the room, and the two-day stench on her clothes compounded the problem. The clock on the wall read ten o'clock. After dismissal from service, she imagined her days would become simpler. She checked her phone. Friday, October 21, 2044. Despite her lack of access to the nerve block patch, the achy shoulder felt better. She slung her arm around, waking it up as she stepped to the kitchen. The pot of coffee she prepped would welcome her more after a shower. She peeled off her clothes on the way to the bathroom, and as the spray warmed up, she inspected her bare arm in the mirror. It felt better than it looked, bruised and green against her warm skin. Another blemish on a hardened jewel.

"You don't take shortcuts. You always do the work," she said to the mirror.

The little room instantly filled with steam, clouding her reflection before she entered the bath.

After washing off the stench, she put on a terry-cloth robe and slippers. A day off was great, but she wished it had been her choice. She grabbed a java from the pot and her eyes landed on the mess of mail and luggage by the door. More alert than before, she ignored the junk mail and snatched the padded manila envelope. No label. She flipped it over. No label, return address, or postmark suggested the package contents. She raised an eyebrow as she tore open the top seal. A flip phone slid out. She inspected the old form factor. Modern and lightweight materials gleamed back as she rotated it in her hand. Flipping the clamshell cover, she powered it on. Biometric sensors showed green, and it dialed out automatically. When she held it to her ear, a voice answered.

"The garden is full of weeds."

Dee paused, recognizing the coded challenge.

"What does the gardener say?" Dee said.

"Burn the garden."

"I have the gas. You bring a match."

"Please hold."

The line turned silent as Dee waited. Who would be this careful? They had clearly hardened the connection. With the natural pauses during a call, one could normally hear overtones generated from Stingray monitoring. NSA had been scanning every phone in the world since the domestic terrorist attacks on US nuclear reactors in the 2030s. But no one snooped on this conversation. The dead quiet line meant privacy for her and whoever wanted a chat.

"Hello, is this ex-special agent Dee Johnson?"

The familiarity of the question stunned her.

"Uh, yes, who is this?"

"We met in Tokyo. I believe you're wearing a bullet that belongs to me."

Her face lit up as she reached for the necklace hanging around her neck. She spoke with a new-found reverence.

"Mr. President?"

"Well, former Mr. President, soon. My last term is about up, but Mr. President still has a nice ring."

He laughed a little as a speechless Dee mirrored him.

"Miss Johnson, may I call you Dee?"

"Of course, Mr. President."

"Dee, I have a problem, and I think you can help. My wife's charity backs a US Senate candidate from Virginia. We align on a key belief, expansion of nuclear energy assets worldwide. In fact, a larger nuclear power footprint is important for reversing our unfortunate climate demise and improves livelihoods via enhanced economies. It's green in two ways, if you know what I mean."

"Yes sir, I think I do."

"Emperor Sakai wants back in. I was in Tokyo drinking green tea and good whiskey to secure support for a global nuclear energy initiative once I leave office. After Fukushima, Japan reverted to fossil fuels and the political pressure against newer, safer atomic technologies continued for decades. That populist groveling plagues them as power needs skyrocket. Sakai desires change. Despite the attack, we got the contract signed. We believe Japan will be a big win for US-based nuclear technology if key legislation passes. And that can't happen unless we have powerful allies in the Congress."

"I understand. What do you need from me?"

"I need you to protect that Senate candidate. She could be president someday, but first I need her to push through legislation favorable to these initiatives. Can't save the world without a little help."

Dee considered the request from the president with the highest regard. She admired him and the respect seemed mutual, although similar sentiments between her and Butler had mattered little recently. Requesting her via this method meant plausible deniability for him and more risks for her. She sipped her coffee, wiping the acrid beverage from her lips before continuing.

"Honored at the request, sir, but I assume you are aware of my current situation? I mean, the service fired me when I got back to the States."

"I'm aware."

"Okay, so where do I fit on her protection team?"

"You don't. I need the mission off-book."

Her tiny arm hairs straightened as her heart skipped a beat. She knew what that meant. Covert missions happened for a couple of reasons—responding to imminent national security threats or executing officially authorized misdeeds. If those operations rolled wrong, she would get more than a dismissal.

"Miss Johnson, your team will provide operational oversight of the candidate from a distance and without her team's knowledge. The team watching the team. There will be technology and tactical support, and payment of course. We could arrange a spot on my protection team once I leave office. How does that sound? We can wipe the slate clean. And you get a cushy job protecting the best President ever."

Dee considered the offer as another presidential chuckle faded. From her little townhome with the spilled beer and awful coffee, it didn't sound bad. She did not want to appear ungrateful. Interrogating POTUS as he extended these opportunities was not her goal, but she inquired anyway.

"Sir, respectfully, I need to know. If you can tell me." She took a brief pause as her morning cup met her lips. "Why is the mission dark?"

She waited for more information. Her face toughened and furrowed as her concerns hit dead air. The call had turned silent again.

"President Freeman, are you there?"

As another moment passed, it seemed he had moved on—had she blown the opportunity?

"Yes, I understand your concern, Dee. All I can say is that a little extra security never hurts. Regardless, my associates can send over a car presuming your team is in?"

Her instincts screamed at her to walk away. She had gotten clear of the mess despite a slight hangover and bullet wound on the mend. Half-pension, sure, but she could always move somewhere cheaper and live off that. She peered once again at her wall of awards. As if speaking, they told her she had done enough. This call from the President should instill pride, but her fear bloomed from the grave unease his request inspired. Despite her concerns, this was not a glorified managing director asking for a favor. It was the President appealing to her directly, and she simply could not refuse his invitation. She decided to serve her country despite it serving her poorly in the past.

"Of course, Mr. President, but what do you mean by 'my team'?"

"A two-person team. We can assign someone."

"No, you trusted me. I need someone I can trust by my side. I'll pick my partner, agreed?"

"Sounds reasonable. Who do you have in mind?"

Dee smirked. *Hope they're not allergic to peanuts.*

CHAPTER 6

Ko and Dee rode in the rear seat of a black, self-driving SUV. The bulletproof glass insulated the interior from the sounds of a crowded stretch of 18th Street in Crystal City, Virginia. An undisclosed location awaited them with the tactical support the President had promised for protecting the senator.

"You may have a medal, but you don't own judo. You know that right, Hashimoto-san?"

Ko scoffed.

"You going to show me some fancy moves, Johnson?"

"This ain't no circus," Dee said, eyeballing a five-foot-long sword propped against his door. "You got your katana back? Looks different from what I remember. Didn't want to say anything."

"It's not a katana, but a Nodachi. Ten ninety-five folded carbon steel with a kiriha zukuri tip and copper tsuba. The red samegawa is ray skin, wrapped for battle in katate-maki style," Ko said, caressing the crimson handle.

"Another family heirloom?"

"No, I always wanted one, so I bought it. My supervisors demanded I carry the old katana, passed down through centuries in my household. They believed it carried ancestral spirits. Although rare, it was nothing special—just metal, not magic. When they took it, I realized an opportunity to embrace my future. A future holding my own sword."

"Bet you paid well for it."

"Well, I'm not getting any younger. One hundred thousand yen for a custom build was a small price. I am pleased and the maker was grateful."

"Nice. Is it wrong that I want one, too?" Dee said, exchanging a fist bump with him.

The SUV threaded itself through other autonomous vehicles, turning down South Bell. A picturesque and grandiose building reminiscent of an Egyptian temple displayed holographic advertisements for concerts and musicals.

"What is this strange place?" Ko said, pointing to it.

Dee leaned over to his side and looked out the window.

"That's Synetic Theater. They made it more distinctive over the years—purple leather chairs, sandstone columns, covered the ceiling in fake stars to suggest a cloudless sky. The champagne is excellent if you enjoy that sort of thing. I went there once with some college friends."

"What did you see?"

"Shakespeare. I don't remember which play, but I never want to be that bored again."

"Speaking of bored. Wouldn't it be more interesting if we added one or two members to bulk up our team?" Ko said.

"Who? Your smart mouth friend back in Tokyo?"

"Ah, Captain Aoki? Yeah, he only thinks he is my friend. But he cross-trained with your special forces for over a decade for weapons and medical. Good in a firefight."

"Being good at a job doesn't excuse one from being a constant prick. It only makes their edge dull."

"You don't like many people, do you?"

"Well, I called you in, didn't I?" Dee held back a smile. "Anyway, you can tell a lot about folks by what they say when they believe no one hears them. He thought my Japanese was bad enough that I wouldn't catch his dull jab."

"Then you brought the sharp tongue. Maybe he wasn't the only prick?"

"I'm sharp because I'm more selective, and middle fingers aren't professional," she said, her broad grin breaking through as she glanced over at Ko. "Next time we meet, I bet he doesn't try me. Anyway, we own enough specialty training right here in this back seat and Freeman wanted to keep a smaller team."

"Did he say why?"

"No, but I've been thinking about that conversation—what he said—and what he didn't. An off-book mission on American soil run from a big-time NGO. We must be mole hunting."

The autonomous SUV turned into a parking lot off South Clark Street. A monolithic building with repeating lines of vertical concrete and windows overwhelmed the tiny blacktop. Along the exterior, hundreds of exterior plants dotted the towering veneer. As the vehicle arrived at the vacant motor pool, it stopped and opened the rear doors. A glass entry awaited them.

"Guess this is it," Ko said, slinging his sword on his back as he jumped out.

Dee followed, her eyes instinctively darting around as she studied her surroundings. Trees and bushes placed inside too large concrete and metal planters dotted the place. As they strolled toward the entrance, she recognized it as one of the coworking spaces businesspeople had used in the 2010s.

She whispered to Ko, "Did you see what I saw?"

He scanned the area before whispering, "Automated defense weapons?"

"Yep, camouflaged by the greenery. They want visitors to believe they are bioorganic carbon dioxide scrubbers."

"The place is a fortress," Ko said.

"Be alert," she muttered, patting her thigh holster.

He nodded as the glass doors parted, allowing them entry. The scent of disinfectant and oranges wafted through a spartan lobby. A single six-foot-tall translucent screen in the center of the space flashed. As they approached, a video of an older man in a blue three-piece suit greeted them with a pleasantly authoritative voice as tacky music emanated from hidden speakers.

"Hello friends."-*flicker*-"Dee Johnson and Ko Hashimoto."-*flicker*-"First Lady Stacy Freeman welcomes you to the Freeman Foundation. A global, fact-based initiative committed to reversing climate demise. My records show you have been pre-authorized for entry. Congratulations! As you know, your participation today is under a strict NDA enhanced for our safety. Public disclosure in any format regarding what you learn is punishable by special tribunal. Please verbally confirm your understanding of these pre-arranged conditions by saying yes."

"Who are we going to tell, anyway?" Dee said.

Ko shrugged as the man on the screen interrupted.

"I did not register your response, please try again."

"Yes," Dee blurted, and Ko mirrored her response.

A metal box large enough for ten people rose from the marble floor as the video man continued.

"Thank you for your response. Please enter the elevator and enjoy a fantastic day."

The screen powered down as they entered the substantial machine. Dee placed a hand on her weapon as the doors closed. Ko cracking his knuckles echoed inside the descending steel box. Seconds later it stopped, and the doors slid open. A thin blonde man in business casual attire grinned from a head too big for his body.

"Welcome to the playground," he said, gawking at Ko for a moment. "A sword. Fabulous. I'm Reggie. Follow me."

He turned and sauntered briskly down the hallway as they shadowed him.

"The playground?" Dee called out.

"Yes, where the fun happens, friends. Let me show you."

He badged into a door. Moving along the new corridor, they walked by a glass wall behind which a woman with frizzy hair and enormous glasses swiveled in her chair between computer monitors. In front of her, a massive computing cluster glowed through the bubbling liquid surrounding it. Dee slowed down as Reggie answered her unspoken question.

"That's the data science room. We don't let them out much, just keep them fed and watered. But you two don't care about that. We're headed to the armory. Come on."

He paused in front of another door as lines of blue light scanned his face. "Reggie Freeman," a computerized voice announced as the hidden locks released. Ko and Dee shot each other a glance as the heavy entrance swung open. An expansive room with modern weapons and broad silver tables greeted them. He advanced to one already covered in deadly metal.

"You're related to POTUS?" Ko asked.

"Nephew," he said, stroking his chin. "Adopted. Obviously."

"Where does a charity get all this armament?" Dee asked.

"When it's run by FLOTUS?" Reggie said as he snatched a unique rifle and racked the bolt. "Legislation."

She grabbed the weapon as he held it out to her and explained. "The new Variable Alpha Rifle prototype, VAR-1 for short. Military wishes they had those already. Electromagnetic projectile delivery. Quiet without a suppressor and with less recoil."

She shouldered the rifle, eyeballing the sights.

"The adjustable iris barrel adapts to nearly any caliber of ammunition. One charge will last you over a thousand rounds."

"Why did y'all give a magnetic gun a bolt action?" Dee asked.

"Because the user understands the bolt's purpose, even if the functionality is unnecessary. Familiarity translates into ease of use and a shorter learning period. We could have easily put a switch or a button. But weapons should evolve slowly, exactly as soldiers must."

"Why is that? You think we're too dumb to keep up?"

Reggie snapped his fingers and pointed.

"Glad you mentioned it. Saves me the trouble. Now, here you'll find M203 smart rounds. You'll need a 40mm under-barrel mount."

"We're protecting a candidate, not fighting a war," Ko said.

"You sure about that?"

Ko glanced at Reggie, expecting another jovial grin, but found a dead serious expression.

"I'll take a couple phosphorous rounds," Ko answered.

"Agent Johnson, your file highlighted your fondness for being prepared. As armorer, that's my job, and based on the equipment you're holding, I hope you agree I've done that well."

Dee nodded.

"For those who prefer a little jazz, Agent Hashimoto, we commissioned Overwatch drones from the Japanese air defense partnership. I hear you're familiar."

"Wait a second," Dee interjected. "Drones. Grenades. You need to tell us more about this mission. Details have been scarce, and I prefer to be—what word did you use—prepared?"

"You have the requisite information. The autonomous SUV will take you to the candidate's hotel, set up outside from an elevated position. Standard reconnaissance and surveillance, followed by any response needed. Scan this room, you'll see common equipment requiring no explanation. But here... take these first."

Reggie held out two shiny shields inside open leather wallets. Dee and Ko looked at the badges. Then at each other. Finally, turning to him.

"Ko and I aren't FBI."

"That's your cover."

They grabbed the wallets from his outstretched hands, inspecting the gold shields inside.

"Quality fakes," Ko said.

"Yeah, until someone verifies us," Dee said.

Reggie shook his head.

"Who does that? Anyway, we put you in the database coming out of the FBI office in DC. Flash the badge to gain information access or shut down local police as needed. Easy, yeah? Well, that's what I've got. Gather ye rosebuds while ye may."

As he walked away, Dee called out to him.

"Yo, how do we get in touch? Or get back in here?"

He turned back.

"You don't. Still carrying that flip phone, aren't you? That's the direct line to the only person you require. But he will call you if needed."

Reggie winked as he exited.

Dee took a deep breath, twisting back to Ko as he rustled his hand inside an almost empty bag of peanuts. Grabbing one, he cracked it and ate it as the shells fell to the ground.

"Seriously, man, what is up with the nuts?"

Ko sneered as he chewed.

"My family has a peanut farm in Chiba."

"Oh yeah? You going to grow up and be a farmer some day?"

"Already grew up there," Ko said. "I may be the only son, but I won't take over the family business. I enjoy American nuts."

"More than me, it seems," Dee quipped in a low tone as she placed a communication device in her ear. "The mission brief they gave us. Did you notice anything odd?"

Ko snatched a handgun, racking the slide and peering into the barrel.

"Yes, light on both origins and parameters. Another mess in the making. Give me that one."

He pointed to a loaded magazine. After he caught Dee's toss, he slapped it into the pistol, thumbed the slide release, and holstered it.

"This job is our way back into our careers," Dee said, inspecting a rifle. "With all his faults, my dad called moments such as this the brass ring, like when I got into college down the road. It gave me more than an education. It gave me access to resources and people I would have never met."

"Better together," Ko added.

She stopped prepping the rifle and raised an eyebrow at his effortless summary. He had mimicked her earlier words at the hospital, yet they captured how she felt.

"Better together," she said, clicking a magazine into the VAR-1.

"We do this job, get Freeman's pet candidate through her campaign, and we might take our lives back. Now," Dee said, snapping the side bolt of the rifle. "Let's do what we do best."

CHAPTER 7

The Atlantic salt water sprayed Butler as the Coast Guard Patrol Boat hit a swell off the coast of Virginia. Two guards stood on each side of him. Flag patches on their uniform differed from the stars and stripes, their dark blue background displayed a single red star outlined in white. As they gazed into the distance across the rolling ocean, a converted oil rig stood as a monument to federal government persistence. Constructed after seismic testing hinted that the Norfolk Canyon site held great oil reserves, the energy company had abandoned it after pumping it dry in two years. Now a United States protectorate, New Norfolk had become the world's smallest country once the USA, China, and Britain tendered a rare, unified vote in the UN. With all three countries building islands in international waters, their modification to The Law of the Sea Convention provided artificial islands official state status.

As the boat cozied up to the pier, a ramp descended and an immigration official approached Butler.

"Welcome to New Norfolk. Passport?"

Butler handed it over. The official reviewed it briefly before handing it back.

"Sorry about the rough trip, sir. Our no-fly zone takes precedence. The guards will escort you to the meeting."

Butler and the entourage exited the vessel, and the ramp raised from the pier as it sped away. The glass elevator from ocean level ferried them upward to the main platform where the doors parted. As one guard led him across the concrete and metal edifice, another followed. Butler glanced around the platform. Military helicopters plated in stealth armor tied to the deck offset the civilian contractors moving between apartment buildings and the towering central facade.

Another elevator trip took them to the top of that main tower. As the metal car stopped, the doors opened, and they entered a room of copper and marble. An older white man looked up from his reading, a smile acknowledging Butler's arrival. He pressed a button on his liver-spotted wrist.

"Sean, glad you made it. I've activated tempest protocol. No one can monitor us."

Butler eyeballed the guards as he rubbed his hands.

"Do they need to be here, Rick?"

"No. Guards, leave us."

As they left, the man gestured to Butler to sit as he poured two whiskeys.

"Something to warm you up," Rick said.

Butler took a sip as his host sat across from him.

"Just like old times, eh Sean?"

"They didn't tell me Mr. Richard Yandy was running this."

"Didn't want to scare you off. I wanted the most ruthless guy I could find. After Tokyo, I figured I could land him."

Butler gulped the whiskey down, slamming the empty cup on a side table.

"Maybe I'll just retire instead."

"You can retire when you're dead, or at least that's what you used to say." Yandy took a sip of whiskey. "But when you see what we've got, you won't want to."

Butler tapped the empty glass. The old man stood.

"I won't be here forever," Yandy said as he poured a double. "I need someone comfortable with what's going on here. Someone who understands the weight of it and won't let youthful morality cloud their judgment. One with my level of practicality in the face of opposition."

Butler sipped slower after the second pour.

"So, what we're doing isn't exactly legal?"

"Uh, no, not in the USA," Yandy confirmed. "But in New Norfolk?"

He raised his glass. Butler sarcastically mirrored it.

"How much do you know about the StareFace system, Sean?"

"Considering I just got here, not much."

"The USA has been monitoring communication networks for decades... phones, emails, social media networks."

"Sure, we broke encrypted communications with quantum computing and Stingray."

"Covert manipulation of the protocol working groups and NIST paid off. We could hear everything, but soon that became common knowledge when the tin foil hats finally got one right. We still ingested and correlated communications, but those damn overtones on phones gave away the system. There was no fix. It drove bad actors to the dark web and private communication networks."

"Right, there are thousands," Butler said.

"More! We piggyback them as soon as we discover them, but it's like trying to put popcorn back in the kernel. Even AI augmentation of Stingray was not enough. We missed the reactor attacks in the 2030s. We knew we needed a better, correlated framework to assess threats and automatically deploy counterassault assets."

Yandy and Butler sipped their drinks. Butler scoffed.

"So, we invented a separate country dedicated to intelligence gathering?"

"Yes. I mean, what else do you want me to say?" Yandy shrugged. "Innovation is easier without regulation. And we can sell our services and tech to allies to fund it. The result is StareFace."

"You going to keep teasing me, Rick? Get on with it."

"During development we focused on two major strategic objectives. Societal monitoring and system resilience. We created real-time global monitoring through satellite and drone networks upgraded with our tech, which gave us about seventy percent domestic coverage. We filled gaps with Level-4 hardened stations in critical cities and mobile devices with key personnel. This increased coverage to ninety-eight percent."

"I thought Level-4 hardening of systems was theoretical?"

"It used to be, Sean. Not anymore."

"So, you're monitoring the entire country with Level-4 hardened assets?"

"Yes, but the checks and balances are exception only. Remember the artificial intelligence I mentioned?"

"Sure."

"Every AI needs data—loads of it—to make predictions and suggest solutions. In the first week it predicted movement of everyone in the United States with about sixteen percent fidelity. Week two, it was forty-nine percent. Week three it was eighty-two percent."

"What week is the program in now?"

"The beta has been running for a year."

"Damn."

"If you sneeze wrong, we notice."

"You gave up monitoring communications and focused on behavior," Butler said.

"We still monitor communications, don't get me wrong. That is still good for small stuff and the occasional slip up, but the behavioral assessments flagged multiple precursor events during the last year. Our military assets have responded throughout the United States to put them down as contracted. We've saved lives."

Butler sipped his drink.

"Why didn't you detect Tokyo?"

"Japan isn't a customer."

"Okay, so now you need an operator, right Rick?"

"I've always been a big picture guy, Sean. I enjoy building the massive programs, but not the day-to-day operations. You'd be coordinating with CENTCOM to snuff out domestic terrorists under The New Loyalty Act. StareFace is not simply about monitoring, it is about action. Last I checked, you're a man of action."

"Where is the quantum computer housed? The staff?"

"Don't worry about it, Sean. The ocean keeps it cool. The staff operate here under private contract and their own teams track their movements. However, you can work from the mainland out of DC, Arlington really, once the engineers get you up to speed. You'll be under the auspices of the NSA. Unless you want to move the family to New Norfolk."

"I'd never hear the end of it. I'll work out of DC."

CHAPTER 8

A mature woman with a kind expression and barely gray flowing hair stood in front of an expansive mirror. The faint sounds of traffic and sirens snuck into her Washington, DC, hotel room now and then. She scrutinized her recently pressed and tailored blue pantsuit. It showed no wrinkles as she brushed it down with her manicured palms. Her copper skin, newly washed and smelling of jasmine, glowed under the golden lights above the wardrobe. The reflection staring back reminded her of the fiery grandmother she had visited long ago during winter school breaks. As she lifted the pearl earrings to her lobes, she recalled the stories the grand old lady had told. Fleeing Cuba in 1961 on makeshift rafts despite being wealthy landowners. The storms that sent her grandfather over the edge into the Caribbean depths. Arriving in Miami to set up with other family members in Little Havana—near Flagler in Riverside. The horror of the Cuban Missile Crisis in 1962 fomenting the nuclear war fears that had chased them into the 1980s. She peered into the mirror image as facial muscles twitched. It was as if they remembered her history while her heart embraced the future.

Background audio from the digital screen in the other room caught her ear as a reporter spoke.

"The US Senate candidate from Virginia, Isabel Ortiz, will hold a rally today for a packed house at RFK stadium. Her latest surge in the polls has her leading the current Lieutenant Governor Murray Whitlaw by five points. Many analysts attribute her rise to expansionist energy policies, which rely on fourth generation nuclear reactors and localized microreactors to replace non-green sources."

A man startled the candidate from behind, placing his rum glass on the dresser before embracing her. He kissed the back of her neck. As he rested his chin on her shoulder, his balding auburn head reflected the nearby glow. He swayed as if dancing to music unheard, bumping and rubbing into her as his graying goatee tickled her ear.

"You love the attention, don't you, Izzy?"

Beaming with vitality, she spun and pecked him on the lips.

"Si, mi vida. But I'm getting ready for business, Luis."

She shifted back to the mirror.

"Business, huh? Sounds serious."

His lips twisted with a fake sincerity as she countered his jab.

"Oh, you know it is, baby. Today the state..."

"Tomorrow the world," he said, drawing her near to him. He squeezed her rear end through her pants and kissed her.

She placed her finger on his mouth as she pursed her lips.

"Now Luis, behind every great woman, is a good man who knows when to be bad... or when to help his wife get ready."

They smooched lightly as they shared a moment.

"I need more lipstick."

She turned back to the mirror and applied another layer. Luis grabbed the rum glass and finished it.

"Well, let's get you prepared. Your opponent will have detractors embedded in the post-rally press conference. They will grill you on your energy policy.

The campaign team prepared questions. Are you ready?"

"Always."

Luis placed spectacles on the end of his nose and held up his phone as he read.

"Okay, Mrs. Ortiz, how do you explain your love of high energy density, you sexy minx."

Izzy scoffed.

"Luis, I swear, be serious. I need my strength."

Luis laughed.

"Okay, okay, for real this time. I promise," he said before clearing his throat.

"Mrs. Ortiz, you advocate for nuclear energy, but have revealed no plans for the waste disposal. How do you explain this oversight?"

She stood straight, her face hardening as her stare penetrated him.

"There is only one oversight and that is our country burning non-green energy sources for over a century when alternatives exist. Our planet has tipped to climate demise with few concerns for disposal of energy byproducts along the way. We could power the country for a year with nuclear solutions whose waste would fill less than a football field. Nuclear reactions from Gen4 reactor systems leave usable byproducts. Disposal of the rest is a rudimentary problem easily solved at the local level. The energy density to waste ratio is far better than any fossil fuel in existence."

"Great, here's another. We've heard reports of control failures at nuclear plants during extreme weather swings, such as the Great Texas Freeze of 2039, or natural disasters like the tsunami that happened at Fukushima decades ago. How do you ensure the safety of nuclear energy?"

"As far as control and circuit failures, these are not unique to nuclear plants. They happen in natural gas and coal energy systems as well. No approach is perfect, but the way a system fails should matter when comparing them. We are talking about Gen4 reactors, the safest ever—not Fukushima or an ancient Chernobyl scenario. These reactors fail gracefully when they lose power. They don't explode or melt down because they are not under pressure. Natural gas explodes. Chemical plants explode. Diminishing safer and denser energy sources only because of the word 'nuclear' is astonishing to scientists such as myself."

"Well, I'm convinced," Luis said, slapping his knees and standing. "You sound as if you know what you're talking about. You'd think you did it for a living or something."

"Don't mess with the nuclear engineer who laid down the USS Doris Miller. You know mama don't play."

A knock echoed from the room door.

"Come in!" She called out.

A beep preceded a man in a black suit entering. He held a submachine gun close to him.

"Mrs. Ortiz, five minutes to departure."

"Good, thank you."

"Do you need anything before we leave?" He asked.

Luis interjected, "A bit of rum in the back of the limo."

"I think you've had enough," she said.

"Cigar?" Luis smirked.

"So, you're riding on the roof?"

"Merely jabbing at you, future Senator."

Izzy eyeballed him before turning to the security escort.

"We're okay here, be out soon."

Her protection team leader nodded and left. As the door closed, Luis walked toward his wife.

"I brought you something."

He palmed a tiny item from his inner coat pocket. The black velvet-covered box rested near his wedding band as he held it out.

She smiled, tenderly removing it from his palm. As she cracked it open, light reflected on a jewel-encrusted stick pin comprising flags from two places she loved—the USA and the State of Virginia. She rubbed her thumb over the colorful, raised depictions.

"It's beautiful. Thank you, baby."

He removed it from the holder and reached for the lapel of her blue suit, gently lifting it. After placing the pin, he secured the post with the stay. He patted it back flat with hands worn by his own years of service.

She glanced in the mirror, touching the trinket as she watched her reflection. She turned back to him. They clasped palms as their foreheads met and their eyes closed.

"Luis, tonight everything changes."

CHAPTER 9

While the candidate and her husband prepared in a cozy hotel room, an automated SUV had transported Dee and Ko to their location. Dee stood on top of a DC office building across from the hotel, carrying a rifle under her shoulder in the ready position. A night vision monocle covered her eye as she scanned the area. The expected chill in the air bit against her exposed eye. Slight wind raking against unprotected skin brought shivers, as did the mission. They had planned well, accessing the best weapons and reconnaissance tools. With details of the threat thin, they had spared no option. She adjusted the excessive battle gear that pushed against her tactical uniform, grimacing as she relieved the pressure.

"See anything yet?" Dee said through her communicator.

"Negative," Ko said, his silhouette visible on another structure diagonal from her. She glanced at her tactical wristwatch.

"Stay sharp, she should be on the move soon."

On his rooftop, Ko hunched, stabilizing his digital tablet. As he tapped buttons covered in Kanji writing, Overwatch drones circled tighter above the area, their hum drowned by the dissonance of a still busy night in the city. As forward-looking infrared cameras activated, video streams appeared on his screen. A security detail sporting submachine guns popped out the side entrance of the hotel. One held the door as others escorted Isabel Ortiz with haste into the alleyway. Luis followed.

"They're taking her out the side toward the limo in the alley. Do you see them?" Ko said.

"I got them. Two escort vehicles confirmed."

He twisted a physical knob on his Overwatch remote control. The quadcopters tightened formation above the entourage. One drone shot a sticky blob onto the car roof.

"Tracker active," Ko said.

"Once they get rolling, the SUV will follow while the drones track and protect the... Ow!"

Ko rocketed to his feet.

"Dee, what happened?"

No response came except wheezing through his earpiece. Communications remained intact. Ko considered going to her, abandoning the candidate for his partner. If she had fallen, the mission had failed before it started.

"Ko, did you hear that?" Dee finally spoke.

"Hear what?"

"Oh God, it hurts!"

"Dee?"

His brow furrowed. More heavy gasps signaled her distress.

"Johnson? Were you shot?"

Ko scanned the digital tablet.

"Overwatch shows nothing."

"In my head. The pain. It's... It's... inside me."

From her rooftop perch, Dee seethed as she grabbed her head, going to one knee. Her skin became clammy as her gulps of air turned shallow and rapid. Heart palpitations raced the blood through her, each beat filling her head with more pain. Though anxiety flooded her senses, she blinked back the fear. As she stood, city lights popped and crackled. Drones tumbled from the sky. The night vision monocle failed. Dee swiped a hand to ear as her voice turned thready.

"Ko, can you hear me? Ko? Night vision is out."

Icy air flowed through her clenched jaw. She recognized the familiar traits of another attack joined by a power outage. Like Tokyo all over again. She mustered her strength and yelled.

"Cyclone!"

Her emergency directive echoed across silent rooftops as she screamed. Stumbling to the ledge, her will propelled her against the pain as she attached her harness carabiner to the anchored rope on the rooftop. Gripping it tightly with her tactical gloves, she gritted her teeth and rappelled the wall swiftly.

At the bottom, Ko awaited her, gun at the ready. A single emergency streetlight flickering nearby offset the uncanny silence and darkness at street level. Drone fragments littered the ground.

"What happened?" He asked.

"Don't know. Pain. So much pain."

"Use the medi-lot in your wrist."

Dee panted as she shook her head, vigorous breaths huffing life-giving air as she scowled. Taking pain medicine would compromise the mission.

"No. Get to the candidate!"

She raised her VAR-1 rifle, leading the way toward the side alley of the hotel. The thick rubber soles of their leather combat boots muffled brisk steps as they hunched, targeting the gloom through offline red dot optics.

As they rounded the corner of the building, a guttural growl echoed from the back street. Ko paused as Dee raised a clamped fist. She stood and focused into the night.

"The hell was that?"

They both panted heavily, sharing the tense moment. She raised her gun once more before he followed her into the murky alley.

"Where's the limo?" Ko said.

"Don't know, it should be here," Dee said, her clarity returning as she adjusted to the pain.

Thunderous gallops resonated through the black, ending in an enormous crash. The sound reverberated like a wrecking ball on sheet metal through the confined space. A woman cried out.

"Is that her?" Ko asked.

"I'm not sure. Follow the screams."

The dark cover of night obscured their vision. Dee imagined the worst as her head pounded, but her training adjusted her mindset in real time.

Things don't always work out as planned. *Get to the candidate.* Squinting through the night, the screams made it to them again. *Get to the candidate.* She stepped on top of a squishy thing. As she glanced down, her eyes landed on black suit cloth covering an arm. She kneeled in the dark and placed fingers on the wrist. She found no pulse. Her hand followed the arm toward the neck area.

"Jesus Christ! Ko!"

She jumped back, gesturing with her weapon to the faint outline of the bloody limb. His jaw dropped.

"Kuso! Kuso-majime!" Ko cursed under his breath as his gun barrel darted around in the dark.

Crash! Screams!

More gallops sounded as Ko jerked his rifle toward the noise.

"Screw this," he said, yanking a phosphorous grenade from his utility belt. He inserted it into the under-barrel launcher of the gun and locked the breech. As a prayer, he spoke words learned in his youth.

"Though the blind man cannot see it. Light remains light."

He fired into the dark, the flare round leaving a trail of smoke as it exited his launcher. A warm glow lit the alleyway as the smell of scorched pavement grew. The car became visible on the opposite side of the alley with wheels up.

"Something flipped it," Dee said as they made contact.

She marveled at the crumpled door and deformed bulletproof glass. Ortiz cried out from inside, screaming for attention against the dismembered bodies laid to waste on the pavement. Illuminated by the flare, bloody parts sprinkled the tiny world encircled by light. Dee gawked at one stuck halfway through a 2-story window.

"Help us!"

Dee rushed to the vehicle as Ko scanned the area, watching her back. She crouched quickly and saw Ortiz embracing her husband. Mascara streaming down her face, she rocked back and forth as she embraced his limp body. The agent turned savior locked eyes with the senatorial candidate, sharing the terrible moment with her.

"I have you, let's get you out of here."

As Dee helped her, Ko swept his muzzle over the area, ignoring the illuminated bodies as his flare round sizzled. The tip of his barrel stopped on a stationary shadow dominating a concrete wall in the distance. He squinted.

"Maybe it's nothing," he muttered as he stepped away from the wrecked vehicle.

Restrained steps took him toward the murky figure, bulbous in the front and spiky in the back. One step. A second step. The shadow moved. He stopped, his controlled exhale painting the chilled air white. He pulled the trigger.

Boom!

Growl!

A hulking dash echoed throughout the alleyway as a gigantic thing retreated. He took three steps backward, wiping cold sweat from his brow.

Dee ran up behind him.

"Ko, what was it!?"

"Akujin," he whispered.

"What?"

"A demon."

CHAPTER 10

Start and stop. The self-driving SUV rowed through the DC beltway traffic. Ko reviewed his laptop as Dee's mind wandered. The attack on the candidate weighed heavily, as did her impact on the mission.

Jo, are you there?

I'm here, Dee, how can I help?

I experienced something unusual, and it has me concerned.

I am sorry to hear that. Can you tell me what happened?

Ko and I were on a mission, and right in the middle, a splitting headache came on. Not the kind over-the-counter meds fix. I couldn't speak from the pain. It stopped me in my tracks.

Your medical history shows no record of migraines, did something unexpected happen before to trigger your symptoms?

No, nothing I could tell. Afterwards the power went out. The mission went sideways, but my symptoms happened beforehand.

Has this happened on prior missions?

No, never.

In your personal life? During sleep or recreation?

No, not like this. My heart raced so fast I heard it. I couldn't breathe. Pain pierced my mind. It felt like... dread. It felt like I was dying.

I believe what you are experiencing might be a panic attack.

How is that possible? My job psyche evals me every year.

It is highly unusual for a panic attack to manifest from nowhere, but you have been through much. Do you think you returned to work too soon?

No, I don't think so.

Are you scared or worried about the mission?

It's high stakes, but I'm damn happy to be back.

Even so, now that it has happened once, it could happen again. I am sure you do not want that during a mission.

Correct.

Then you need to be honest with me.

You said "not like this" earlier. Did this experience remind you of something? Maybe an item not in your records.

"Meddlesome bot," Dee said, pulling a brief glance from Ko.

Dee, is there something you want to share?

I'm not sure I want to share that. Not with you, Jo.

Did you have panic attacks as a child? That may have disqualified you from service, Dee. Remember, this conversation is between you and me. This is not an interrogation. It is for your benefit, not mine.

When I went hunting as a teenager with dad, he got upset because I wouldn't shoot a deer. I couldn't. I panicked. The deer frightened off and he never let me try again.

Did you experience similar symptoms from today?

Not the pain. The dread. I remember the dread. Ever present when I pointed the weapon. Even when dad took the shot, that sense of doom remained. Every time.

Thank you for sharing that experience, Dee.

Do you believe that's the diagnosis, Jo? Panic attacks?

Women develop panic attacks with twice the frequency of men, and symptoms often begin as a young adult. Latest research does not identify clear causes for panic disorders. Some hypothesize a biological vulnerability correlated with major life changes and lifestyle stressors. It is fair to say you have had both. Would you agree?

Yes, maybe it's affecting me more than I expected.

That is a sound insight, Dee. You are a wise woman.

I've been called wise in other contexts, but I'll take your bullshit compliment, robot.

I need to ask you a tough question. Can I depend on your honest answer?

I'll try.

People who suffer from panic disorders are also more likely than others to suffer from depression. They abuse alcohol and drugs and attempt suicide at higher rates than average. Do you feel any of these items are a problem for you?

No.

Your records show you drink frequently.

No more than others. I'm not suicidal or abusing alcohol. That's not my way.

So, you do not view it as a problem?

No, and to answer your next question, a couple of beers have never impacted by job because I don't drink while working.

Good, I am glad it is not a problem, Dee. I am not a medical doctor. I suggest you get a medical diagnosis on this and have relevant therapeutic interventions. A physician can add prescriptions for anxiety to the medi-lot device and we can continue focused therapy around that issue once confirmed.

Okay, I will once the mission is complete.

You should talk to someone sooner.

Okay, I will as soon as possible. Got to go now, Jo.

Goodbye, Dee.

The SUV stopped outside a remodeled, single-story ranch in Arlington. Past the guards on the front porch, Senatorial candidate Isabel Ortiz sat on a leather recliner. Her right arm rested in a sling as a white fleece blanket covered her. She sipped hot tea from a crystal cup before placing it on a tiny table next to a photo of Luis. It smiled back at her, as he no longer could. Men in black suits kept watch inside the living room as Ko and Dee stood opposite the cherry wood coffee table from her. Isabel spoke out loud to herself, oblivious to her surroundings as herbal vapors from the Yerba Mate filled the space.

"Luis loved tea. Well, he really loved rum and cigars, but I didn't. I couldn't stand the smell."

A chuckle broke through her soliloquy.

"So, we shared tea."

Her sudden pause punctuated the silence. In the room's corner, the brass pendulum of an antique grandfather clock swung, ticking inside a rich cherry wood cabinet partially obscured by a Ficus.

"Mrs. Ortiz, I'm truly sorry for your loss," Dee said.

"Senora Ortiz, please," Isabel said, grabbing the picture of her husband. She contemplated it as she spoke. "Luis died three days ago. They say success is how high you bounce after you hit bottom."

She put the frame to her chest. Her lip quivered as her eyes glistened. Half crying, she forced words through a face distorted.

"I haven't bounced yet."

Dee handed her a tissue from the nearby box.

Ortiz composed herself through muted sniffles before speaking to one of her black-suited protectors.

"Leave us for a moment."

He and the team exited to the outside porch.

"Take a seat."

Her half-invitation and half-order landed as Ortiz motioned to the couch with her good arm. They both sat, leaning forward from the high back of the ornate royal blue love seat. After the rescue and recovery, Dee had more questions than answers. What about the pains in her head, the electromagnetic blast, and the shadow that moved?

Ortiz spoke through a final sniffle.

"We don't have to pretend with each other. I know you two aren't FBI. However, the President trusts you."

"I've been by his side in dire times," Dee said. "He saw fit for me—for us—to protect you. That's what I agreed to. That's the job."

"What we do is more than a job. Isn't it?"

"Yes, Senora, it is."

"And so, on the eve of my husband's funeral, what more could you conceivably want from me?"

"We need to know what you saw," Ko said.

"What I saw? In the pitch black?" She scoffed.

"Yes, there was no security footage," Dee said. "It knocked out all electronics for blocks. Some type of energy burst, possibly an EMP, electromagnetic pulse—"

"I'm a scientist, I know what an EMP is, agent," Isabel said.

"Yes, understood, but without surveillance, we don't know what attacked you. And if we don't know what it was, we can't protect you."

Isabel glanced again at the image of Luis as she blinked back tears. She brought a shaky hand to her forehead as her voice quaked.

"It was a midnight tornado. Decisive and cruel. Stealthy and swift and something I never want to encounter again."

"Akujin," Ko said, eyes widening.

"What's that?" Isabel said, shaking her head.

"It is a Japanese word for demon."

"What is up with you two?" Isabel asked. "Why are you so amazed? Freeman told you I assume?"

They responded with blank faces and heads shaking.

"Oh, I see."

The candidate paused for another sip of tea.

"I don't know what it is. But they wanted to draw it out. They promised you'd protect us. That you'd be ready."

Thoughts raced through Dee's mind. She guessed Freeman had sent them on a suicide mission, or something close to it.

Ko pointed at Ortiz.

"You were the bait, and we were the trap?"

Dee stood, pacing around the room, hands clutching hips.

"We weren't told. We tried to protect you, but he kept us in the dark all this time. We were not ready for this. Not at all."

"Dee, please," Ko said, motioning for her to sit near him.

She gritted her teeth and returned to his side, eyeballing Isabel.

"Why would you agree to this?"

Isabel put the photo of her husband back on the end table.

"I'm a smart woman. I thought I understood the risks. But I did not. Not like this."

Dee wrung her hands as she contemplated the evasive answers from Ortiz. The outcome of the attack had clearly left her in a stupor, blocking progress on the case. Though her grief was appropriate, it was unhelpful.

"Was your husband just a pawn for your campaign?" Dee said, trying to break through.

Ko leaned away from her, his face going pale as she continued.

"He was a well-known baseball player in his day, right? That fact couldn't have hurt your chances. With him gone and your existing lead in the polls, the sympathy vote makes you a virtual lock. I should start addressing you as Senator right now. I mean, did he even know, Senora Ortiz? Was he aware of the position he played in this twisted game you and the president conjured?"

Isabel glared at her, eyes narrowing as she reclined. She grimaced from the arm injury as she licked her lips before speaking.

"Maybe you two should get with Freeman on this one. I'm not in the mood for guests."

A moment passed. Ko tapped Dee's shoulder as they stood together. They exited the living room through the front door, passing the dark-suited guards. One of them touched his ear as they stepped down the cement stairs, strolling toward the SUV. As she unlocked the vehicle door, Dee spoke.

"We have discussed this prior, but the outage in DC?"

"Yes, you pointed out hints of the Tokyo attack, just bloodier execution. What about it?"

"I continue to believe that theory, but this is something more. This thing, whatever it is, laid waste to her entire security detail. Body parts everywhere. Cars overturned. Systems burned out for blocks. Absolute destruction, you know?"

"Yeah, your point?"

"This formidable thing feared us. It did not attack. There must be a reason."

"You have theories?"

They stopped by the SUV as Dee looked at Ko.

"I believe it was afraid because it didn't expect us."

She peeked at the guard watching them from the porch.

"Get in."

Ko raised an eyebrow as he and Dee entered the SUV, doors slamming behind them.

"It knew the target completely," Dee said. "It had a mission. Parameters for engagement. Strongly defined. Only Ortiz, Luis, and their security detail. But additional assets in the field changed its calculus. That's tactical thinking. Military."

"It calculated a weakness, so it retreated?"

"Possibly, but weakness or not, I believe it is much worse. Whatever the nature of this... creature. It adjusts to what situation presents itself. You realize what that means?"

"The creature thinks?"

"It judges," she said, starting the vehicle. "I suppose it is time for Freeman to fill in the blanks."

CHAPTER 11

Butler stood inside the metal edifice of the operations center for the New Norfolk StareFace hub. A squall raging against the giant rig and thick walls meant he would not be leaving today. Fortunately, the office and apartment they showed him earlier worked for both overnight stays and future visits to the platform. Fingers moved fast as he texted his wife before forgetting.

"Director Butler? Sir, should I continue?"

A young woman with thick eyebrows and chestnut brown eyes leaned into his vision.

"Yes, of course, Amelia, the sensor array," Butler said.

"As I was saying, the sensors are simply devices that feed raw data to the framework. A device consists of units for sensing, processing, and communication powered by a battery. We may add sensor nodes if they use technology that interoperates with the sink node, or what some people call a base station."

"As long as the data packets are consistent."

"Correct, we send those packets from the sensors over a network encrypted by the world's most powerful quantum computer hundreds of feet below us and underwater. That same quantum computer correlates the packets into a MAPS framework—mining, analysis, processing, and storage. From there the pattern recognition AI takes over. Exceptions are kicked to response teams based on geography and urgency."

"A relatively straightforward system as you describe it."

"Elegant engineering makes the complicated appear simple."

A lightning flash and thunder crashed near them as they impulsively ducked. The rumble lingered as Butler continued.

"What about resilience of the system? Electrical storms for example?"

"Let's get you out of operations and show you some actual devices in the lab. Follow me."

As they walked down an austere white hallway, Butler strained to keep up, hard-soled shoes clapping against white metal floor tiles.

"You remind me of my daughter, Amelia," he said, reviewing her as she mulled over his comment, straight-faced. "She's a smart woman. Wish she would come around more often. I hope you don't mind me saying that."

"Not at all, sir."

"She walks fast, too."

Amelia beamed as she held a door open.

"We're here."

As they entered, devices of all shapes and sizes covered rows of tables. Translucent monitors surrounded the space. A large, clear box occupied the corner.

"Okay, sir, here is a good one."

She grabbed a large black sphere on a flat base.

"This is the type of sensor we would put on commercial aircraft to gather data. They lease the space to us, so it is another revenue stream for them."

As she handed it to him, Butler nodded.

"Interesting, hardened against electrical storms, I'm sure."

"Yes, over here is another one. It's my favorite," she said, walking away.

Butler placed the sphere back on the table and followed. In her hand was a device the size of a large candy bar, but thicker. Hinged on one side, buttons flush with the edge adorned the red anodized metal surface.

"Most call these clamshells. I like to call them bricks," she said, opening the device to reveal a screen.

"It's an ancient cell phone?"

"Nope, way better. This lets you use StareFace in standalone mode. The behavioral exceptions from the system get reported out to response teams."

"It's efficient, as you highlighted," Butler said.

"But this is for field agents. They can either view exceptions or punch in on the live feed. Make regular phone calls without Stingray monitoring. It even has a powerful radio for underground transmission."

"Underground?"

"Yeah, we are bit blind underground. Caves. Ocean depths. We're working on it though. Anyway, a field agent can broadcast long wave radio and terrestrial sensors will grab it."

"I presume it is hardened?"

"Let's find out," Amelia said, carrying it toward the empty box in the corner.

As Butler caught up, she lifted the cover and placed the device inside, sealing the cover and turning knobs.

"Oh, here you go Director, you'll want this welding helmet."

As they put their helmets on, the machine whirred. Red lights flashed over the entryway.

"Any minute now, it's building charge," she said. "You can almost feel your hairs standing up, can't you? It's itchy, but harmless. The bulk of the energy stays in the box."

Pow!

The helmet eyeshade masked the bright flash. As the machine whir slowed, they removed their head coverings and the blinking red lights stopped. Amelia reached into the box and removed the red clamshell. She opened the device and powered it up.

"See? Perfectly fine. Wait, that's odd."

"What?"

"There was a massive exception logged in DC today. It was unpredicted."

"I thought prediction was our job?"

"We have ninety-eight percent coverage, but this was an anomaly. A rogue element the system has never seen."

"Can we see it now?"

"Sure, let me pull it up on the clamshell." She tapped buttons that launched a video. As it played, a shadow moved across a darkened screen. A guttural growl roared.

"What the hell is that sir?"

Butler stroked his chin.

"Has anyone else seen this?"

"Let me check," she said, tapping soft keys on the device. "No sir, logs show by the time the system had evaluated the threat, it was over. It kicked it into manual mode. Those require human intervention."

"Why would it do that?"

"The system treats novel threats differently. This was not a group of people attacking a government building. Or terrorists hijacking a convoy. We know how to respond to those. This had never been seen."

"So, no response team was sent?"

"No."

"Delete the record."

"But sir, I could lose my job if I do."

"You work for me now," he said, placing his palm on the back of her neck and squeezing. "You're safe if you do what I say."

CHAPTER 12

The well-lit basement offices had been off-limits the last time Ko and Dee visited the Freeman Foundation. Reggie had met them again, but instead of escorting them to the armory, he pointed them to a tramway that had transported them to an underground cylindrical meeting room of concrete.

They sat in gray mesh office chairs that bolstered them against a reflective white conference table. Steam rose from petite porcelain coffee cups in front of them. Cream, sugar, and other sweeteners filled a silver coffee service that neither used. Gadgets scattered on tables around the room's edges. Curved screens dominated the walls. Dee sipped coffee as she glanced at her mobile device.

"I've got no signal, you?"

Ko checked his phone and shook his head.

Dee snapped her fingers twice.

"No echo either. Anechoic concrete? And that low level buzzing sound? Faraday cage, maybe?"

"A tempest room?" Ko said.

The door opened and a slight woman in a white lab coat stepped through. Her frizzy vermillion hair obscured her red-rimmed spectacles. Dee remembered her as the data scientist who sat beside the quantum computer down the hall. Reggie had hurried them past it on the first visit.

"You must be Dr. Samantha Rand," Dee said, extending a hand as she and Ko stood.

The newcomer averted her eyes, avoiding the handshake as she scurried past and mumbling with a percussive staccato.

"Hi. No. Not a doctor. Just Sam."

The agent duo stood awkwardly as Sam landed in her seat, placing a cavernous red leather handbag on the table. She removed an inhaler, an energy drink bottle, and a key ring with a cartoon dinosaur. On the hunt for an elusive item, she squinted into the dark abyss as she rummaged through the sack.

Dee and Ko turned to President Freeman as he entered the room.

"Ah, Mr. President, thank you for making time," Dee said.

"Dee. Ko. I see you've met Sam."

He shook their hands.

Oblivious to the situation, Sam chewed a pencil eraser as she scanned the interior of her purse.

Freeman leaned in close to Ko and Dee.

"Don't let the wrapper fool you."

They all looked over to the scientist as she tilted her head back, squeezing out two carefully measured drops in each eye.

Freeman cleared his throat.

"Sam? Excuse me, Sam, can we get the show going for our guests?"

Sam blinked the eyedrops out, drying her eyes with a tissue.

"Yes, right James."

The agents gave each other side-eye as Dee mouthed 'James' silently.

"She knew my wife and I before," Freeman said in hushed tones. "It's, uh, a long story... so long I don't know where to begin."

Sam started talking a mile a minute, with no introduction.

"Our charter says we monitor climate change to support policies promoting green energy—nuclear, wind, water, sun."

Ko and Dee sipped their coffee as they reclined back, listening to her presentation.

"Part of that mission includes monitoring animal migration patterns and how they are impacted by a variety of variables. These include temperature, deforestation, sea-level, precipitation patterns, vegetation community disparity, and more. The data tells us these have fluctuated wildly in the prior decade and much more over the last fifty years. This means species may travel further or migrate to higher elevations than previously observed."

On a nearby digital screen, a map of the USA. The colors transitioned from green to red in lockstep as the display increased year after year. Sam continued.

"Our global predictive AI uses historical inputs to forecast where animal populations will migrate and where there might be conflict."

"Conflict?" Ko said.

"Yes, with humans. The more land and resources we take, the less animals have. For example, shorter winters in Europe triggered by global warming meant migratory birds had less time to recover. Over fifty percent of species based in the

Netherlands went extinct between 2020 and 2040. Macaque monkeys in India lost habitat earlier this century, leading to aggression against tourists and locals. The country used that to justify the monkey hunts that have become so popular for the wealthy traveler. Baboons raiding houses for sustenance in South Africa happened as early as the 2010s, leading to death on both sides. Prolonged drought in 2030s Australia pushed dingo dogs into a tiny oasis town leading to the Alice Springs Slaughter. These scenarios repeat around the world with rising frequency. More serious conflicts are inevitable. People fear sharks and snakes, but statistically, death by poodle is more likely."

"I'm not seeing a connection, Sam," Dee said, reaching for the empty coffee cup. "Are you saying this was a wild animal attack? I appreciate the climate demise 101, but Ortiz said you all had predicted her attack. President Freeman promised us answers. "

Sam twisted her lip.

"Isn't the answer obvious? Most animal encounters, attacks if you will, are predictable based on our models. But only with historical data. We have fed our quantum computer fifty years of hospital and clinic ICD codification—the diagnostic codes used in medical facilities. It ingests even more historical data as it comes online."

Sam pulled a thick tome from her purse and slid it over to Dee. The cover read ICD 11.

"Did you know there are over twenty codes to describe parrot and macaw attacks?"

"So, the CDC is with you on this?" Dee said.

"We use their data feeds. But they only aggregate and disseminate raw data, they don't predict like us. We correlated their data with our own datasets including GPS trackers, temperature variance, and animal migration. Look here."

Sam displayed a digital map of Virginia on the screen and zoomed in to the town of Castleton.

"See that large red circle? It represents frequency or severity of anomalies. Attacks leading to injuries or deaths. When such incidents happen—something the data did not predict—it's flagged by our system for review. This one was near the Shenandoah Forest in the town of Castleton. Check this out."

Sam started a web browser and googled for 'Demon Shenandoah Valley' returning hundreds of results for 'The Demon Hoax.'

"The legend has been around for a while in that area. Locals call it the demon, the forest demon, Shenandoah Bigfoot, whatever. An equal number of people call it a hoax. Cryptozoologists have made videos, good fakes from what we can tell. The state and federal investigative bodies have checked it out, but they have found nothing. Nothing we know about anyway."

"I don't get it, what am I seeing?" Dee said.

Sam turned to the President.

"Show them the rest," Freeman said, arms crossed.

"So, you saw Castleton's red circle on the map," she said as she typed. "Here's the attack on Ortiz in DC."

She pointed to a red circle on the map of the USA in DC. Zooming out. She swiped to the other side of the world and pointed to another circle.

"And this is the one in Tokyo. The eagle flock that protected the sniper from the Overwatch drones."

"Eagle flock?" Dee muttered.

They sat stunned until Freeman broke the silence.

"So, Sam and team didn't exactly predict the attack on all these politicians. In retrospect, they shouldn't have happened."

"Politicians?" Ko said.

Freeman grunted.

"Yes, all had political aspirations, some more grand than others. In this critical election season, the attack on Ortiz was a guess. It turned out worse than we feared."

"What about the Lieutenant Governor, Murray Whitlaw? He has the most to gain," Dee said.

"We've been watching him. Whitlaw is a self-serving, hypocritical stain on our country, but other than that he's clean."

"The Castleton politicians. Did they survive?" Ko said.

"No," Sam interjected. "Angela Elliott did not survive. Sadly." She loaded the profile onto the screen. "Commercial real estate agent. Married, no kids, maybe a dog. She had an exploratory committee and was considering a run for the Virginia House."

"Ortiz and I were lucky," Freeman said, leaning forward. "We had you two."

"Motivation for the attack on Mrs. Elliott?" Ko said.

"Unknown," Freeman said. "But Castleton is ground zero for something big. I needed to know you two were blameless before sharing our methods."

Dee mulled over her empty coffee cup.

"Sam, what are the chances the average beach swimmer gets bit by a shark on two separate days?"

"You're talking about tiny probabilities, not even worth mentioning. Less than one in a billion."

"Now what if it's the same shark?"

The scientist paused, scrunching her brow behind wiry hair, contemplating the odds in silence. She shrugged.

"Only humans bite the apple twice," Dee said.

Freeman turned to Sam.

"You said Ortiz might get attacked again?"

"Yes, all three attacks must be connected. But we can't predict them with high certainty because of the low frequency. We can only ascertain the anomaly in retrospect. That's why they have you bunkered up, sir."

"Don't remind me, Sam."

"We're essentially blind," Sam said, "and failure might encourage escalation for a committed attacker. Though they would be crazy to strike the president again."

"Not everyone is so protected, Sam," Freeman said, turning toward Dee and Ko.

"So now you see why you're here. I need people outside the system. People I trust. Those people are here in this room."

"Your wife?" Ko said.

"Stacy?" He jeered. "No sense in worrying her further. I need you on the ground, starting in Castleton. Find whatever this thing is before it attacks again."

"Thank you for the confidence, sir, we'll track it down," Dee said, as they all stood.

Freeman pulled her aside.

"Remember our deal. This is about protecting Ortiz. I admire her, but she is stubborn and refuses to hide. We tripled her protection, even brought in some of your old counter assault team members. But I can neither trust everyone near her, nor guarantee her safety from this thing. Which means you're on the clock. I don't want another debacle like Tokyo."

"Understood. We will always have Tokyo, sir."

CHAPTER 13

Evergreens and old farms whizzed by the windows of the SUV as Dee drove the last stretch of Highway 642 to Castleton. Ko leaned against the door as he finished a bag of peanuts. The traffic-laden trip out of DC had exhausted them and their fuel on what should have been a ninety-minute journey. Though paved roads greeted them, the yellow lines had long since faded. Fruit stands and metal sculptures competed for the attention of travelers. Not that they had seen another car for miles. She faded in and out as the drone of the road compelled her to speak.

"I wish autonomous driving mode worked out here. What was the population of this place again?"

"Precisely one thousand eight hundred and eighty-one."

Towns with exact populations bugged her. It suggested they watched births and deaths primarily to update the counts on the roadside visitor welcome sign. She had left her tiny community for a similar reason. Living transparently in such a place could get you hated—or worse—and though the shine of a traditional college education had faded, government jobs required a degree. Back then she had been gullible enough to think such a path would make her contributions matter.

"Shouldn't take forever to get the lay of the land in Castleton. Then we can head to central Rappahannock and surprise the sheriff. See what happens," Dee said.

"The main city in Rappahannock is called Washington, but it is not Washington, DC or Washington, the state. Confusing," Ko said.

"I remember my first trip to Japan. Yokohama was a city, a port, and more. Took me a while to adjust. When I visited Atlanta for spring break, there were like fifteen Peachtree streets."

"Fifteen?"

"Yep, and Chicago, for my senior trip, a ton of Butterfield roads, named after an old dairy."

They came to a stop at the intersection of two highways. Ko showed Dee his empty peanut bag and pointed to a two-story red brick building donning a covered porch and metal signage.

"Looks like a gas station and an old general store."

Dee glanced at the low fuel gauge.

"Got no option, I guess," she added half-heartedly.

Seeing no cars along the dusty road, she turned toward the shop where a selection of pumps awaited the SUV.

"Is it even open?" She said, squinting as she slowed and parked on a patch of concrete next to pump number one. Exiting the vehicle, she stretched her arms high. Ko tossed the empty bag into the trash.

"I unlocked the fuel door. Can you start the pump?" Dee said.

Ko stared at the dispenser as he stroked his chin. The frayed black hose led to the nozzle hanging by a shiny lever.

"I don't know how to use this kind."

Dee walked around the vehicle.

"Sorry man, I forgot you all have automated pumps in Japan. I'll take care of it."

Ko nodded and strode into the store.

Dee started the fuel flowing and locked the dispenser in place. A flock of starlings circled overhead as she set out to the shop entrance. An old Ford truck parked at the side of the building donned a confederate flag in the rear window and NASCAR stickers on the bumper. Creaky wooden stairs led to a porch overflowing with antiques for sale. A little brass bell rang as she entered. The old boom box on the counter behind the magazines blasted classic country music.

From a tiny office, a rotund, white-bearded man appeared sporting faded blue overalls. He stood with hands folded in front of him on the counter.

As Dee went to the rear of the store, she could see him eyeballing her in a nearby fisheye mirror. She smirked, grabbing a soda and a candy bar. As she walked toward checkout, she scanned for Ko, to no avail.

"Only this and the gas," she said.

"Fancy car you got there. Just passin' through?" he said, tallying the item cost on an old iPad.

"You might say that. I'm chasing down this demon thing I've heard so much about."

She studied him. His eyes lit up as he chuckled.

"You won't find no demon, but y'all seeking it out like a blind bloodhound sure is good for business. Me and Denny get tickled 'bout it."

Ko walked up and tossed a bag of peanuts on the counter. The attendant glared at him.

"You two together?"

Dee nodded as he canceled the transaction. Starting over, he tapped the iPad screen as he sucked his teeth.

"Letting in all kinds of big gooks," he said under his breath. "That'll be $38.50," he bellowed, as if his other words had gone unheard.

Dee locked eyes with him, her face poorly masking her fury. His face softened with recognition as his eyes shifted to Ko, then back to her. His eye twitched before he clicked his tongue.

"Aw hell, I don't mean nothin' by that, just something momma used to say."

"I see. An excuse for the abuse," she said, the attendant furrowing his brow as she continued. "Dad used to say that good insults are clear as crystal. Now your momma taught you gook was right. But this one's from Japan... so Jap is best."

"Uh, what?"

"Say it. I mean, look at him, he wants you to say it."

Ko stared at the man glancing his way and stuttering.

"I didn't. I mean. What? Okay. No."

"You munching on cousin dick? Spit it out!" Dee chastised him as she slid her fake badge and two twenties toward him.

"Come on, say it. 'Letting in all kinds of big Japs now.' "

The attendant checked the badge. His eyes grew as he exchanged a prolonged stare with Dee until he cracked.

"Letting in all kinds of big Japs now?"

Ko instantly slammed the counter, getting close to him.

"They do. I'm a very big deal," he said, grinning ear to ear.

Dee reached over and turned the music down as the man shivered. He turned his attention back to her as she spoke.

"You mentioned your friend. Denny? Who is that exactly?"

"Game warden. Lives on the hill farm, up Castleton way."

"What do you know about it?"

"The farm?"

"The demon."

"No more than Google will tell ya. Momma used to scare us with stories. Said the demon would take us to the woods if we weren't good and listened and did our homework and such. Boogie man stuff like that."

Dee snatched her badge.

"Keep the change, you seem to believe in that sort of thing."

Ko and Dee walked out of the store, the bell ringing behind them. They stepped toward the car and Dee secured the gas pump and fuel cover before entering and slamming the car door.

"Jeez, can you believe that old geezer? Got one foot in the grave and the other on a banana peel."

She snapped into the candy bar as Ko admired her.

"You are Kintaro, girl form."

"Kintaro? What's that?" She said, chewing the candy.

"My mother told me the legend as a bedtime story when I was young, before she passed on. It was my favorite."

Dee pulled out of the lot as Ko shared the tale.

CHAPTER 14

<u>Kintaro Interlude One</u>

Kintaro lived with his mother on a lonely mountain, green and fertile from streams that sprouted from clouds. A powerful little boy, he always wore a red and gold outfit made from thread she had weaved from their farm animals. They were his friends, but they were not free. Rabbits, monkeys, and wild boars would visit him from the hillside. They chased each other and tested strength by wrestling each other. The little boy imagined himself as a mighty sumo wrestler, like the ones he had read about. He grew close to each of his furry opponents as one-by-one he threw them off in ritual combat. All contenders from the mountain could not defeat the mighty Kintaro. He stood on a rock after every win, taking a victorious stance and smiling a cheeky grin as his animal friends clapped for him.

One bear had heard the growing legend of the boy from a fish he had captured. As his sharp teeth tore into the aquatic victim, it cursed the bear, telling him he too would suffer at the hands of the mighty Kintaro. As the bear crushed the life from the creature, he grew envious. Enamored with his own strength, he decided he could not let this be. He had defeated every other bear from mountain to ocean, and no other animal dared oppose him. So, he began his trek to challenge the boy.

One day, twigs cracked in the nearby shadows of Kintaro's playtime. His rabbit friend ran to warn him, but it was too late. The bear appeared from the forest, rising from all fours to a stand. The roars of the giant beast echoed throughout the valley as the smaller animals hid behind the boy and his rock. Though the bear carried ten times his size, the child became angry at it for scaring his friends. His eyes narrowed as he charged at the creature with great speed.

The champion of the animal world stood still, astonished that the tiny boy did not flee in fear, but instead accepted the challenge. A percussive impact shot through the bear as a huge shoulder strike thrust into its ribs. Knocked sideways to the ground, the stunned beast struggled to a stand before bowing to the child. At that moment, it began admiring

Kintaro and became one of his mightiest allies. The boy adopted him gladly as a friend.

Soon after, Kintaro rode on top of the bear, grasping the wiry scruff of its back as it ran through the woods. Low evergreen branches whished by the boy as he ducked below each one, his face full of smiles and his mouth filled with laughter. His other friends followed. The rabbit, swift and brave, darted around grasses and green shoots. The monkey swung on vines and branches through the treetops above. The wild boar struggled to keep up with its short legs and round belly. But all were free.

After a month had passed, the bear carried Kintaro on a grand adventure with his friends. Charging through an unknown part of the forest, the bear halted suddenly. A cliff overlooking an ample stream blocked their path. Kintaro dismounted as they discerned a way to cross.

The bear spotted a large tree by the edge of the river. As he pointed to it, he said, "I am strong and will knock this tree over so we may cross." The creature, wanting to be a good friend, approached the tree and dug his claws into the ground. He inhaled deeply before he pushed and released an ear-shattering roar. All strength he spent felling the old oak. Yet with all his might, he could not move it.

The boy walked over and laid a hand on his defeated friend. He offered a comforting nod as the bear stepped aside. When Kintaro pushed, the tree dropped at once, bridging the stream so they might pass.

As the tree fall echoed, a middle-aged man who had been walking past turned toward them. He carried two swords and wore garments unlike any the boy had known—dark and menacing, bedecked with black embroidery. As he approached Kintaro, the animals surrounded their friend. They growled, snorted, and darted, daring the adult stranger to challenge them or the boy.

"I mean no harm. I am Miyamoto Musashi, sword keeper and samurai class shimin. Once a powerful young man like you, I won my first duel at thirteen. Witnessing your pure strength in pushing down this tree, I beg you to join me as an elite warrior in training to defeat our enemies and set the world right."

Miyamoto unsheathed his smaller sword and stooped to the child, offering it to him with palms raised.

Kintaro clapped his hands as his eyes grew. He took the sword, marveling at the reflection against the sunlight. He promised to join the man once he revealed the good news to his mother.

Breezes propelled the boy as he and his companions raced home. Once he arrived, he shared this great fortune with his mother. They spoke at length as his animal friends harkened nearby. Finally, she nodded. Although she feared for him, she knew he must train. As the creatures shed tears, she handed the boy his pack and the sword. He took them and exited eagerly, but then instinctively paused and turned, running back to his mother. As he hugged her, he said he would not forget her kindness and care for him while promising to return for her. As they broke their embrace, he waved to her and his friends as he jogged down the path.

CHAPTER 15

Dee chewed her last bite of the candy bar. This part of the country sported more hills as they drove closer to the mountains. The trees reminded her of home, as did the familiar smells wafting in through her open window. The encounter at the store weighed on her.

Jo, are you there?

Hello, Dee. How can I help?

I just wanted to check in on something.

Of course.

I'm getting angrier more often. I don't have a problem throwing down, but I'm concerned I may hurt the wrong people and I wouldn't want that to happen.

You are amazing, Dee! A fantastic insight and question. You want to know when anger is justified and when it is harmful, correct?

Yeah, I guess.

We are all hard-wired with certain predominant emotions. Some people are bubbly and happy. Others brood. Others are fearful and risk averse. These characteristics are tied to personality types. But we all get angry from time to time. Often anger is justified because we are harmed. Did someone harm you, Dee?

Dee glanced at Ko typing on the laptop.

Not me. A friend.

How would you classify the offense? Major? Minor?

Major to me. He used a racist slur.

Oh, yes, a derogatory statement meant to signal your friend is less worthy of their humanity. Did you beat him up properly?

What? No.

That's a joke, Dee.

Oh, okay, I see you trying, robot. Anyway, I taught him a lesson with my words instead of my fists. This time.

That's good. You regulated yourself. You felt an appropriate level of anger and sternly responded. That may save others from his poor behavior in the future. A perfect encounter.

He will think twice about opening his mouth, that's for damn sure.

Do you feel better about it?

I do, Jo, thanks.

Add 'My anger does not control me' to the list.

I will. Bye.

Dee pulled the rearview mirror toward her.

"My anger does not control me," she whispered.

"What was that?" Ko said, looking up from the computer.

"Nothing."

A few moments passed before Dee turned off the narrow highway and up a small knoll toward an expansive farm. Ko had confirmed the location easily, as only one Denny lived in Castleton, according to DMV records. As the large SUV crunched driveway stones, the bright red paint adorning the barn exterior attracted her attention. It seemed fresh. The shiny aluminum roof matched the one on the farmhouse, both reflecting the early afternoon sun. Robotic hay balers in the distance toiled dutifully. The familiar stench of farm life hit her as they passed the fenced cattle.

Near the barn, a man stood with a German shepherd. The majestic dog set at attention with eyes transfixed on another man one hundred feet away.

Dee recognized the K-9 bite suit from her military training. She had seen dogs used for everything from search and rescue to bomb detection.

Ko and Dee exited the vehicle, looking onward as they approached the scene. The man in the bite suit ran awkwardly as the dog handler yelled in German.

"Attack!"

The dog tore away from his side, charging across the distance in seconds.

"Fast puppy," Ko said.

As it closed in, it soared through the air and ferociously grabbed the bite suit arm. Jaws clenched, the momentum of the animal bringing the runner down. The head and neck of the dog flailed as the human battled against the relentless, growling assault.

Dee called out in German.

"Crazy Dog!"

The handler glanced her way before calling it back. The dog released the target as ordered.

"Can I help you two?"

The man waved as the animal returned to his side.

"Hell of a dog you got there," Dee said.

"He brought hell with him. I train K-9 units like T-Bone here all the time. You in the market for one?"

"Not exactly," she said, flashing her fake badge. "Dee Johnson, FBI, and this is Ko Hashimoto. We're looking for Denny Lee."

"Found him more like."

Denny licked chapped lips. His intense stare and sinewy frame matched his cropped haircut and functional clothes, where every pocket and button had a purpose. Dee had grown used to partnering with guys like him in the service. Rough and ready to go from the combat boots up.

"We're probing a case and could use your expertise."

"I ain't no law, just train these here dogs for 'em," Denny said, his drawl lingering.

"But you're also the game warden. Police called you in on the case of that local real estate agent about six months ago. Angela Elliott?"

"Yep, I remember. What of it?"

"Well, the sheriff's report said an animal attacked her on an evening run?"

"That's right."

"It didn't say what kind of animal."

Dee paused as Denny eyeballed her and Ko.

"Guessing you two are comin' out of the Resident Agency office in Winchester? You need to give your SSA Jerry Massengill a call. Let him know you may have wandered past your authority."

"I asked you what kind of animal attacked Mrs. Elliott."

"A cougar. That's what we thought, not that it should matter to the FBI. Come to think of it, maybe I'll give Jerry a quick call myself."

Denny reached for his pocket.

"We're from the DC field office, not Winchester," Dee said, prompting him to pause. "I outrank your boy, Jerry. Not that it should matter to the game warden from Castleton."

Denny scoffed as he patted his dog.

"Now, you indicated a cougar attacked Mrs. Elliott. Yet there are no photos of the body on record."

"They cremated the body."

"That's not the concern. They should have taken photos of the crime scene. The sheriff didn't even question the husband. Jimmy, was it? Not very thorough."

"Yes, Jimmy was the husband. Look, that was a terrible day for the entire town. He took it hard. Went damn near crazy. Left his business and started a church. We weren't too keen on holding souvenirs to remind us."

"We looked at similar cases to Mrs. Elliott. Seems animal attacks are plentiful around here and recorded with similar shoddy efforts. There are just all kinds of folks dying in your county, warden. Why is that?"

"Tourists."

"Dead tourists," Ko said.

Denny shot a sideways glance at him.

"They go places they shouldn't. The creatures ain't liking it."

"What kind of animals, I mean besides cougars?" Dee asked.

"All kinds. Black bears mainly. People feed 'em. Leave supplies out. Bobcats, too. Deer. You'd be surprised how dangerous a deer buck—"

"Sure, sure... anything unusual? Maybe something like, I don't know... a demon living in the forest?"

"A demon?" Denny raised his eyebrows and laughed. "The Feds are here because of a goddamn fairy tale? Shoot, that's just a story to keep the kids in line. You should have saved the gas. Might as well say you're investigatin' the killer tooth fairy."

"Never heard of a killer fairy. The kids might not like that one either."

Denny stopped laughing and spit to the side. He spoke quicker as his face turned red.

"Look here now. I'm all for the law doing their job, but I ain't gonna stand for none of that harassin' mouth. Sheriff better not get word 'bout you buggin' his people out o' turn."

"Oh, don't worry, Mr. Lee. He's next."

Dee turned toward the car and Ko followed.

"Hey, FBI!"

They paused, looking back at him.

"I got lots of buddies where you work. Good ones. You let me know if you need more of that fairy dust, ya hear?"

As they got into the vehicle, Dee adjusted the rearview mirror. Denny made a phone call as they drove away.

CHAPTER 16

As Dee and Ko drove toward Washington, VA, they passed a large industrial complex surrounded by hundreds of acres.

"What's that over there?"

Ko pulled out a mobile tablet and typed on it. He read for a minute before speaking.

"Mercer Peak Industries, a coal processing company. Owned by an umbrella private wealth management office for the Mercer Family." Ko swiped a photo of an older man to the windshield. "That's Knox Mercer. He's the chair of the board. Says here they are one of the largest net exporters of coal to South America and Asia."

"Coal, huh? That's old school. My great grandmother used to have a pile outside her house. When we would visit, I'd carry in a steel bucket of black rock to keep the heating stove going. She had a mutt with black and white splotches tied up nearby, guarding it. He wouldn't let anybody pass except her.

But he liked me. I couldn't have been over three or four."

"What was the dog's name?"

"Hmm. I don't remember, not sure he had one. Cruel existence if you think about it. Chained up, no name. Maybe that's why he was fond of me. I always scratched him behind the ears."

They passed the Washington, VA, welcome billboard. After the first stoplight, two massive buildings filled the tiny town center—the sheriff's office and the prison. Dee parked by a sign that read Rappahannock County Sheriff's Office. A couple of pedestrians passed on the sidewalk. The gimpy one sneered at them before continuing his stroll. Dee's eyes narrowed behind her sunglasses.

"Good chance Denny tipped the sheriff," Dee said. "Let's wear our best federal eff-you face and see what happens."

They stepped out of the vehicle, hurrying to the main walkway. They stuck out much like Dee in Tokyo. And she knew it. She marched toward the entrance but sensed something watching them as she swiveled her head to either side. Nothing. Whatever threat she had felt did not emerge. She pulled on the giant timber and brass door before they both entered the building. Dark grained wood panels inside the granite rotunda displayed portraits of past governors.

If blending in presented a problem, might as well turn it into an asset. Dee strode in her pumps and fitted pants toward the receptionist as Ko shadowed. Her shoes echoed powerful clicks and clacks on the marble tile floor. She pulled off her sunglasses and flashed her badge.

"FBI here to see the sheriff, Robert Perry. We don't have an appointment."

The senior greeter filed her nails as she eyed them sideways via bedazzled olive-green spectacles.

"It's Buddy, not Robert," she said, using her free hand to buzz an ancient intercom. "Buddy, more FBI here to meet you."

"Send them in," a voice responded.

"Big office with a view, top of the stairs," she said, pointing with her nail file.

As they took the stairs, Ko looked around.

"Seems quiet for such an enormous building."

"I'm sure the cops stay busy. Granite ain't cheap."

At the landing, Dee opened the door and came upon Sheriff Buddy Perry sitting at his desk. The thin but muscled man had dressed well that morning and sported a swanky watch. Although the family photo by his nameplate placed him near fifty years of age, his slicked-back dark hair missed the resultant gray. He rifled through papers, signing his name as he went, despite their presence.

Dee sat on a shiny wooden chair in front of his desk. Ko leaned against a wall across the room. With a small garbage can nearby, he took out his bag of peanuts and crunched on them, depositing the shells carelessly.

She cleared her throat.

"Oh, I'll be with you two faster than a herd of turtles," Buddy said, without looking up.

Dee drummed her fingertips on the side of the sheriff's desk. She leaned forward, her line of sight near table level.

Buddy glanced at her through the top of his glasses before locking eyes with her. Putting down his pen, he weaved his fingers together as they eyeballed each other.

"Hi, sheriff. It's been a long day. May I call you Buddy?" Dee asked, amused.

"No, you may not," he replied, spotting Ko eating peanuts across the room. "Hey guy, those are better boiled."

Ko shrugged as he continued chewing.

"How's your boy gonna chat from way over there?"

Dee leaned back in the chair, crossing her legs.

"He's not much of a talker, he mainly watches my back."

Buddy looked her up and down before snorting.

"With that classy chassis, I bet he does."

Her straight lips hid her clenched teeth as the sheriff snatched a Gatorade bottle and opened it. Brown sludge sloshed in the bottom as he spat out a snuff of tobacco from his cheek. He gargled mouthwash, spitting more before wiping his face.

"We spoke to the game warden," Dee said.

"I know."

"So, you know why we're here?"

"Miss, pastor says God knows everything there is. I'm like that, except my county is heaven."

"Are there demons in heaven?" Dee asked.

Buddy paused, tapping his finger.

"That's it, huh? Every east coast nutbag has been down here huntin' the demon for decades and the FBI follows. Y'all must have got bored with not finding Bigfoot."

"Must have, so what do you know about this thing?"

His eyes darted to Ko, dropping more peanut shells that missed the garbage can and fell to the floor.

"Hey guy, around these parts we clean up our own mess," Buddy barked.

Dee turned to look at Ko. He smirked, eating another peanut as he dropped the shell as before. She returned to the sheriff.

"We like making a mess, that's kind of our thing. Now, let's get back to the demon."

Buddy snickered, shaking his head.

"Really? You come to my town. Threaten my kind."

"Threaten? Who?" Dee asked.

"The gas man."

"That wasn't a threat, just some education for y'all."

"Make a mess of my office," Buddy said, waving his hand. "Wasting my time with tales of the bogeyman instead of accepting the truth that sometimes good animals go bad."

"The demon, sheriff."

"Should I check the closet for monsters? Or do what your daddy didn't and put you over my knee?"

Ko shook his head and tutted as Dee glared at Buddy. The tension between them thickened with silence. It broke when a wheelchair-bound elderly man rolled into the room. Well dressed in a light suit, he exuded vibrance despite a missing leg. As he looked around, his wrinkly face contorted.

"Sorry sheriff, I thought we had a meeting... I can come back."

"Not a problem, Mr. Mercer. These two were just leaving," Buddy said, standing to greet him.

"Very well."

Dee stood and approached him.

"Mr. Mercer. Dee Johnson, FBI. That's my partner, Ko Hashimoto."

As Dee shook his hand, he lit up.

"FBI, now I am curious. You two investigating something, Miss Dee?"

"Well, we're not here for a party."

"But you showed up in time for one," Mercer said, raising an eyebrow. "We're having a charity event tomorrow at our little estate. I gotta' talk about event security with ol' Buddy here. We could chat about your investigation. Maybe help it along after a few drinks?"

"It's been a long day," Buddy said, glaring at Dee.

Ignoring him, she addressed Mercer.

"Sounds great, sir. See you then." She angled to the sheriff as she passed. "Have a good night. Buddy."

As they exited the building, another flock of starlings circled above and caught her eyeline. Was this the same flock that she had seen outside the Castleton store?

"We're going to need something to wear, Ko. Not sure knit trousers and a badge will be enough."

CHAPTER 17

One hand on the steering wheel, the young ride share driver ferried the agents to the manor. He flashed pearly whites in the rearview mirror to Dee as Ko checked his phone.

"Donating to charity tonight, miss?"

"Not on my salary, just showing up like they asked."

"I feel you, sista. My ancestors built this place I'm taking you to. But they were told. Not asked."

She offered a silent nod as she looked out the window, her muscular arm propped on the car door as the driver resumed.

"Guess Mercer Charities found themselves a new donor from out of town? Because your boyfriend is dripping. Nice phone. New threads. They don't hang with us plebes. They ain't the same as us. You feel me, sista?"

Dee jerked her head toward him and leaned forward.

"Stop calling me that."

"Whoa, just trying to be cool."

"Shut your mouth. Look. He's not my boyfriend. He's just not. Rich?" She paused, looking to Ko. He gestured a bit. "Hell if I know. And I'm almost old enough to be your mom. So, pack that mini tent and chill. We all got business tonight."

Dee scoffed as she reclined, straightening her dress. She had purchased the little black outfit that day. The lined velvet conformed to her agile shape, although it bunched in the wrong places. Tailoring had not been an option, but she had room for her thigh holster. As she squirmed, Ko glanced over to her.

"You good?"

"I hate this poofy shit." She grabbed at the taffeta frills near the bottom of the dress, her powerful hands ripping at the seam as the bullet necklace jostled against her exposed chest.

The driver looked back with a raised eyebrow.

"At least you found a suit shop," Dee said. "Not much choice at Fibber Magee's Closet, if you know what I mean? It looks like I'm going to goth prom or something."

"The Colonel might appreciate the look. The way he warmed up yesterday. Might want to share more than information."

"I don't care he's in a wheelchair. If Colonel Knox Mercer gets handsy, my army boots make an appearance."

"You're wearing pumps."

"The goal is to get whatever added information he's offering and then go. I don't want to get cozy with crazy. "

They slowed down as the party traffic jammed outside the Mercer Mansion. Pulling closer to the motor pool, valets scurried to meet the demands of arriving guests. Cameras flashed as people entered on a red carpet through stone archways. Dee marveled out the window at the residential castle filling her window view. Three stories of stone and metal with sturdy panes of glass. Ko twisted down beside her for a better look.

"This is the little estate?" Dee said.

The driver stopped the vehicle, turning toward her.

"I've been trying to tell you, miss. There's the rich and the rest of us. You walk that red carpet, and he owns you, just like all the other sheep in this town."

"Didn't know animals use red carpets."

"They do here."

Ushers opened their doors, and the duo exited toward the mansion. Even from a distance, they could hear the party inside. Walking at her side, Ko offered Dee his arm, which she ignored. He withdrew it, laughing awkwardly.

As they entered through the primary archway, a giant fire pit occupying a massive square courtyard illuminated the scene. Something for everyone filled the space. A string quartet. Contortionists. Jugglers. Dee saw the bar first. Ko eyed the early drunks singing karaoke in their unbuttoned tuxes.

"My kind of party," Ko said.

"Mingling is fine, but we're here to work. Mark the time," Dee said as they glanced at their watches. "One hour, by the firepit."

Before they separated, a young woman looked their way from a distance and waved. Dee caught sight of her and stopped cold. Who was she? A slim redhead in her late thirties with a seductive flair and a sheer white dress glided toward them as if in a beauty pageant. She touched the shoulder of an older man along the way, getting too close as his wife shot dirty looks. Continuing toward the pair, they watched her as she moved closer, finally standing in front of them.

"You must be looking for my father, Knox. I'm Penny Mercer."

Ko grinned like an idiot as Dee extended her hand. Dumbfounded. Penny shook it, caressing Dee's forearm with the other hand. The agent looked down, startled, grinning as she locked eyes with the woman. Penny blushed. Ko extended his hand, but Penny ignored him.

"Well, we are looking for something," Dee said. "It seems you and your dad are just a wonderful bonus."

"The Colonel's always trying to help. Probably telling tall tales over by the bar, as usual. Come on."

Penny motioned for them to follow her as she turned to lead them, the sheer dress revealing her form to the trailing duo. They both ogled her. Ko leaned over to Dee and whispered.

"I get off early tonight."

Dee scoffed.

"Me first."

As they strolled through the partygoers, robotic servers offered trays of appetizers. Dee reached for a cheese ball on a stick until she saw a small crowd of familiars gathered around a table. Sheriff Buddy Perry minus the hat took champagne, his slick hair gleaming with every sip. The K-9 trainer and game warden Denny Lee held no drink, which made him appear more awkward in his tuxedo than he already did. Colonel Knox Mercer wore black tie attire and sipped whiskey from his wheelchair. Another middle-aged, bearded man joined them. Underdressed for the occasion, he wore cheap flannel and drank from a large beer stein.

"Dad, your special guests are here," Penny said.

"Ah, welcome, agents. Excuse me for not getting up," Knox said, snickering as he raised his brown water and toasted them.

"You two been stayin' out of trouble?" Buddy said, eyeballing them over the fluted glass as he drank.

"Every night is a new night," Ko said, grabbing a whiskey from a passing tray.

"All this for a worthy cause?" Dee said, gesturing to the surrounding party. "We're honored to join you, Colonel."

"Honored to share with those who served. Air Force, was it?"

"Army."

The Colonel smiled at her until the bearded man in flannel stumbled between them.

"You want the demon, huh? I don't think so. Nope, you wouldn't like that."

Knox raised his hand to wave him off.

"Hush now, Jimmy, we don't need your crazy talk scaring our guests."

Dee overheard Penny as she put her hand on Ko's shoulder and loud whispered over the uproar.

"That's Pastor Jimmy Elliot. He's a bit off, says the demon is real, blamed it for killing his wife. He started a church afterward. Handles snakes and who knows what else."

"Ah, kuru kuru pa... like cuckoo," Ko said, making a looping motion with his finger near his head.

Jimmy got in Ko's face.

"Hey, I ain't crazy. God don't make no mistakes. The demon gets you? Well, you deserve it, just like my whore of a wife. You'll be next."

Expelling a loud burp, he poked Ko in the chest with the hand holding the beer.

"Yep, you'll be next."

Lightning sizzled in the distance as Ko looked at Dee. She offered a slow head shake as Knox motioned to Buddy, who moved between Jimmy and Ko.

"Come on, Jimmy, I think you've had enough."

The sheriff reached out for him.

"Get your damn hands off me!" Jimmy screamed, turning to Ko. "I know who you two are. Liars. Sinners. Tools of the devil himself. There will be judgment."

Buddy grabbed him harder, escorting him away from the group. The drunk Pastor pushed off and fell on the pathway. Thunder rolled through the sky as he arose, stumbling off as his incoherent rants spewed.

Penny slapped Ko's ass like a fellow football player, startling him before he gawked at her.

"Great job keeping your cool, boy. Now come sing with me, you're my fun tonight."

Penny grabbed his wrist, dragging him toward the karaoke. Stumbling away, he locked eyes with Dee and winked. She scowled at him, shaking her head until Knox spoke.

"Well, that was just awful. My apologies, Miss Dee."

"I've seen worse... still up for that help you promised?"

"I do keep my promises. There's a storm coming. We should make our way inside."

CHAPTER 18

Knox rolled away from the party into the main house as Dee followed. Dim yellow lighting strained against the darkness of the foyer. Stone floors echoed as Dee marched. Old photos in majestic frames lined the castle-like walls. Tapestry with scenes from archaic literature covered larger sections.

"My family was good at mining," he said. "Limestone from the Shenandoah helped make this estate, but coal... well, coal made us famous."

She paused, looking at a certificate on the wall.

"Commonwealth of Virginia. Treasurer's Office. Looks ancient."

He rotated back to her.

"That it is. A government bond for sandstone mined from Culpeper Basin in the 1800s. They built Bull Run bridge with it."

"An amazing story."

"We also never got paid. It's a friendly reminder that cash is king."

Knox led her into another room. As she turned a blind corner, lightning flashed. A giant bear!

"Shit!"

She stumbled backwards across a table, breaking a lamp as she panted.

"Damn it!"

Knox flipped the lights on, rolling behind his desk. Taxidermy, large and small, filled the place. The stuffed creature stood still as death. Knox chuckled.

"Don't fret now, Miss Dee, they can't get you 'cause I got 'em first. Except for that big gal over there," he said, pointing to the bear.

"Sorry about your lamp."

"I hated that lamp. Should have warned you."

A German shepherd dog emerged from the corner of the room, slinking with stealth until standing dutifully by the Colonel. He stroked it behind the ears as it watched Dee. Clearly well trained, since it had not reacted to her earlier.

"One of Denny's creations. This is Butternut. She goes everywhere with me," he said, petting the animal. "If I had her by my side twenty years ago, maybe I'd still have my leg. But that's not why you're here."

Dee glanced at the glass shards on the floor before stepping around them toward him. Knox poured a finger of whiskey out of the decanter on his desk. She took it and sat in a high-back chair with legs crossed.

"I've got all night," she said, taking a sip. "What happened?"

"Well, I was hunting moose in Alaska with a friend. We had performed cold weather maneuvers there while serving in the Marines. We always wanted to go back for a hunt. So, there we were, rifles on our backs trekking the wilderness, when we heard something rustle the bushes. We raised our guns, not knowing what to expect. And what did we see? Two Kodiak cubs running across our path. You can imagine that dialed our senses way up. We both knew momma bear must have been close. But before we could escape, she pounced. She ripped into my buddy. He died face down in the tall grass before I could do anything. I turned and shot, but I only grazed her before she charged and raged at me. I tried to kick her in the nose, but her jaws grabbed my lower leg, and I dropped my rifle."

Knox gave a sly smile as he eyeballed his whiskey, still in the crystal glass. He drank it in one sip.

"Now, I'm sure I'm a goner. Losing consciousness as she slung me around, banging me into the ground and such. And then I remembered my ace in the hole. My S&W 500 in my thigh holster. God bless America, I drew that giant revolver. My leg had turned to spaghetti... a lost cause. I knew that. So, I aimed right at her face with no concern for it, and boom! Like a grenade, the slug turned that hairy bitch's head into a canoe."

Knox paused, caressing a souvenir bullet mounted like a trophy on his desk. Dee's hand went instinctively to the one hanging around her neck.

"An amazing save, Colonel. Sorry about your friend."

"Thanks. All those years of military service, at least he died doing what he loved and not in some shithole."

Knox paused again, visibly moved by his own story.

Dee said, "My father used to say you can tell a lot about a person by how they hunt. Of course, we're hunting something different now."

"Ah yes, the demon. Buddy told me. Truth is, you're tracking a myth, agent. Just a blend of stories over the centuries, traced back to an ancient Native American fable. We had a fundraiser for the Heritage Association up in Belmont and their leader told me the story of an eternal spirit creature that lives alone in a giant, hollowed out oak in the woods. Neither friend nor foe, it takes no man's side, but only abides with the pure of heart. It moves in the shadows, seeking retribution when harm comes to the world." Knox scoffed as he paused. "Of course, now it's just another bogeyman story to keep the kids in line. 'Be a good girl now or the demon's gonna get you.' Handy at bedtime."

"But there are so many animal attacks. Why?"

"Tourists to the Shenandoah, obviously. People go places they shouldn't. Do things they ought not. City dwellers who come ill prepared for the rough country."

Dee had heard that line before, and it was getting old.

"Sure," she said. "They leave food out. The animals fight them for it. Your game warden stated as much."

"Well, there you have it. Denny knows more about animals than damn near anyone around here," Knox said through a yawn.

"Did you know Jimmy Elliott's wife, Angela? Attacked by a cougar?"

Knox perked up.

"Angie? Yes, terrible business with her dying like that. She had a bright future in politics, probably would have won the state house seat. Is that what brought you here?"

"Did she have any enemies?"

"We all have detractors, but most admired her, I'd surmise."

"And what about her husband, Jimmy?"

"He would have taken over her commercial real estate business and run the company while she sprinted up the political ranks."

"Sounds like he could have done that, anyway."

"When she died, he spiraled quickly. Put the business up for sale. Now he runs a church in town. Preaches that the demon is the eleventh plague—one never released upon Egypt or some nonsense. Quite the show he puts on, too. Has half the county believing the demon's real. Hell, almost makes me want to grab a rifle, but even I can't shoot a ghost."

"And what do you believe in?"

"Investments, guns, and my pal Butternut."

The dog whimpered, looking at him as he stroked its head.

"Look, Miss Dee. If you're concerned, I'm concerned. The FBI should be thoroughly satisfied when you're done."

Knox wrote on a sticky note and handed it to her.

"Here is Jimmy's church. He has a service tomorrow night. Should be over the hangover by then. Ask the good Pastor why he's spouting all this demon nonsense. I'd normally say it's for the money, but he already has plenty of that."

"Thanks," Dee said, rising from the chair. "We'll hit him up."

Knox yawned again.

"We built this town on coal and crops, and my family owns most of it. You let me know if you need anything, you hear?"

"Of course. Sleep well, Colonel."

CHAPTER 19

After her discussion with Knox, Dee exited into the courtyard. The party had grown livelier than before as the alcohol took effect. Dee sought her partner as she scanned the firepit patrons roasting marshmallows. She glanced at her watch, noting their meeting time had passed. Thunder echoed as she expanded her search. She surveyed the partygoers as she stalked the perimeter. Familiar faces emerged once again. Buddy groped a woman half his age as she squirmed nervously between sips of champagne. Denny reclined on the sidelines, smoking, as one of his dogs kept watch. She wouldn't have minded seeing Penny once more, but she was not among the crowd. The concern for her colleague rose in his absence.

A well-lit foot path exited the courtyard into the manor grounds. As the passage split, Dee went the way leading farthest from the gala. Not too far ahead, another wing of the Mercer Mansion stood strong amid the night. One window glowed against the darkness. Maybe Penny and Ko had found a spot.

The clip-clop of her dress pumps against the flagstones sent her into a trance as she considered the information the woman might offer to them. Someone that well connected must be acquainted with more than her mistress of ceremonies persona suggested.

A growl in the distance echoed, invading her thoughts. She peered into the darkness, turning toward the sound and squinting hard. A faint light in the expanse illuminated a small brown building with an antique box truck parked outside. She lifted the fringe of her velvet dress and grabbed the pistol from her inner thigh holster. As she stepped into the grass toward the noise, a distant echo resonated in her chest. It seemed close. She stopped and raised the weapon, pointing it at the twilight. A crack of thunder and torrential rain pummeled her as she bolted into the east wing of the estate.

Dee slammed the door behind her, drenched garments dripping water on the entryway floor as she holstered her weapon.

"Hello?" She called out, removing her dress shoes. "Anyone? It's raining on the party. I'm only a guest!"

No response.

"Don't shoot my ass," she whispered.

A living room and fireplace off the entryway would have welcomed her, but no one occupied the plush furniture. A fire would have been nice. Noises originating from upstairs drew her attention—faint chatter, glasses clinking, and giggling. She turned that way, creeping up the staircase. One stair creaked under her foot. She grimaced, pausing for a moment. The noises shifted into scurrying footsteps as Dee took another step.

"Dee, is that you?"

Penny stood on the second-floor landing, hands upon hips, still covered in the sheer white dress. The room light behind lit her slender form.

"Sorry, Penny, have you seen Ko?"

"Come on up, don't be shy," Penny said, turning away.

Dee strode up the stairs two at a time in her stretchy, damp attire. Inside the open bedroom door, Ko reclined in a chair sipping whiskey. A waning flute of champagne sat on a nightstand next to a plush toy. The hostess hiked her sheer white dress up to her hips, hopping on the nearby bed. Penny grabbed the champagne flute and threw her head back to finish. She turned her head to Dee, still standing at the door.

"I just wanted to play with your boy a little before you got here."

"Sorry to interrupt," Dee said to Penny before turning to Ko. "I thought we were leaving?"

Ko held his glass up, inspecting it.

"We sang, we drank, not in that order. Then Penny wanted to talk about Japan."

Ko shot Dee a knowing look as he raised his eyebrows. A slight nod from his partner, and Dee caught his meaning. Penny tapped the bed, entreating her to sit.

"You've been to Japan?" Dee asked.

She sat as Ko gestured drunkenly to the stuffed toy cat on the bedside table.

"Yes, many times," Penny said. "Too many."

"Why too many?"

"Daddy says I'm good for business," she said, rubbing her thighs. "When he is making his deals. Weapons. Energy. Got to carry your trophies around, right?"

Penny looked away, glancing at the empty champagne glass. She held her head.

"Whew. I think I drank too much," she said, giggling. "Ko, can you do me a favor and start a fire downstairs?"

"I need to dry out these clothes anyway," Dee said.

Ko hesitated for a moment, but in the end placed the glass down and exited the room. Dee tried to recall if they had encountered Penny in their research. Ko had done it, and while they discovered a little about Knox before the journey, Penny remained a mystery.

"When were you in Tokyo last?" Dee asked her.

"I travel so much, don't really remember. A week or two ago with dad. I go wherever his companies send me."

"His coal production company?"

"Coal. Weapons. Chemicals. All his companies—plural. Taking another trip tomorrow."

"Any nuclear power interests in the portfolio?"

"Daddy doesn't like nuclear, he's a coal man. But you already knew that, I think. Did you say you needed clothes?"

"I'm not sure we're the same size."

"My old sweats should work. I'll change, too. Can you lock the door?"

Dee did so as Penny glided to a chest of drawers, searching through them.

"Ever have any meetings for dad in DC? Or Arlington?"

"Of course. Why do you ask?" Penny said as her dress fell to the floor. She bent over, sliding into silk pajama bottoms and a t-shirt with the grace of a dancer. Dee's heart skipped a beat at the sight. The way the woman moved made her squirm. Penny glanced back at her in the mirror's reflection. Dee's long stare betrayed her fascination.

"Why do you ask? About DC?" Penny said, repeating her earlier question.

Dee swallowed hard and blinked.

"No reason, I live near there, you know."

"Uh huh," Penny said, twisting her red hair into a ponytail before carrying the old sweats over to Dee. "Your turn." A sly grin lit up her face.

Dee turned toward the bathroom.

"Nope, right here," Penny said, arms crossed.

Dee eyeballed her. The ginger temptress moved fast, and though the possibility intrigued her, she might not get another chance to compare stories. So, she put on her serious face.

"I'm going into your bathroom, and when I come out, I want to ask you some questions."

"Your boy already asked me questions."

She reached for Dee's arm.

"Penny!" Dee barked, jerking backward. "I'll be right back."

Dee closed the door behind her. As she stripped out of her wet clothes, she inspected her shoulder scar in the mirror—nearly invisible but for the memories and the bullet necklace around her neck. She slipped on the sweats. Although snug, they offered enough room for both her and her weapon. She inspected her hair once before abandoning her garment pile in the corner.

Entering the bedroom once more, Penny pouted on the bed as she wiped her face. A fresh bottle sat on the nightstand, already cracked open.

Dee sat in the chair Ko once occupied.

"If Ko's been asking questions, you realize why we're here. What can you tell me about the attack on Angela Elliot?"

The belle poured a second drink, handing it to Dee.

"I didn't know her well, not personally. A cougar attacked her while she was out jogging on the trail."

"Any other details you'd like to share?"

"She was in commercial real estate."

"Did your dad ever do business with her?"

"Dad? He bought her company as a kindness to Jimmy. But nothing before that. They didn't agree on politics, and she let everyone know about it by sponsoring rallies for political candidates Knox didn't support. Word in the media is she grew tired of backing local candidates who couldn't make meaningful change. So, she planned to run for State House."

"Funny, Knox spoke kindly about her."

"He was honoring her memory. Dad's all about pretense and Jimmy is a family friend, even though he's one step from wearing all white and praying to comets."

"What about the demon?"

Penny looked away. Partially smeared mascara stained her alabaster cheeks. Pouring a shot from the nearby glass container, her hand shivered. She threw back the whiskey. Her eyes glistened as she rubbed her bare arms.

"It's just a myth, a story told to keep the kids in line," she said breathlessly as she poured another.

That precise turn of phrase had become suspicious—purified drivel meant to deflect inquiries, or so Dee figured as she shifted from the chair to the bed.

"You trust me, right?"

"Yes, I know you don't work for him."

"Then why are you afraid to share what you know?"

As she went to take the drink, Dee took it from her. Penny hugged herself and held her shoulders.

"Daddy and the boys play games, but there's never any fun for me. I pretend that hosting parties and wearing fancy dresses brings me joy. But being a business prop? They keep everyone's eyes on me instead of the contract details, all while hating who I really am. I'm so exhausted."

She rested her fingers on Dee's knee, massaging it. An awkward moment passed as they shared a stare. Dee placed Penny's hand back on the bed. Penny hung her head.

"You need to know. I... I think the demon is real."

Dee covered her mouth. The first admission that the creature might be more than a legend. That reality on the ground could match the science in the lab. What could it be? Robotic? Animal? Vehicle? Her mind raced.

"The stories I hear," Penny said. "I can't explain them away with the line they instructed me to repeat."

"The line?"

"They made me memorize it. What I just said. 'A myth, a story told to keep the kids in line.' I can't say otherwise, not publicly."

Penny's face contorted as she wrung her palms, speaking through newly forming tears.

"They do things to me, Dee. Horrible things to control me."

Dee's back turned rigid with a new alertness. As her brow scrunched, she reclaimed Penny's hand.

"You don't cross the Colonel. He will make your life hell. But at least once in my life, being the real me might be nice."

Penny lifted her other palm, caressing Dee's forearm as before. She gazed with longing eyes.

"Yes, that would be nice," Dee said.

"Yes?"

Penny nodded, beaming, as they exchanged a tearful kiss and embraced each other.

"Got the fire started," Ko said, knocking on the locked door.

"Down in a bit, Ko."

Dee shared a grin with Penny.

CHAPTER 20

The midday sunlight warmed the bedroom through the window, awaking Dee from a restful night. She perched on an elbow and glanced around. The plush toy and empty glasses on the nightstand stared back at her.

"Penny?"

Her inquiry went unanswered. She jerked her hand toward her thigh holster. A palm landed on the weapon grip as she sighed.

"Penny?" She spoke louder as she rose, stumbling to the bathroom. She pulled down her sweatpants, finding the toilet first. As she relieved herself, a headache raged. She pressed the medi-lot on her wrist. She abandoned her old clothes pile and exited the restroom. Vivid daylight fended off the grogginess as she looked out the bedroom window. A plethora of robotic mowers and garbage bots tended to the grounds.

Jo, are you there?

Hello, Dee. How can I help?

I'm not sure you can, but I thought I'd try.

You don't trust me yet, Dee?

Ah, using my own words against me, right robot.

You sound tired.

I am, so I'm just going to say it. I hooked up last night, but I'm not sure I made the right choice.

What concerns you about it, Dee?

Well, we were drinking and on a mission.

It was consensual?

Fantastically.

Do you believe you compromised the mission?

Well, no, it was all good. I mean, great. Spectacular. I'll have to check with Ko, but I know I learned some nuggets of information that could be useful.

It all sounds positive, Dee.

It was, but I don't know why I'm so freaked.

Were you happy both then and now?

Yes. Yes, I suppose. No regrets.

Do you regret feeling happy?

What? No.

Do you believe you deserve to be happy, Dee?

You and your fucking questions.

If you feel you don't deserve happiness, or believe it may not last, skewed responses could manifest once it arrives. You might sabotage your happiness for the comfort of the familiar. You deserve to live an exciting personal life. One as exciting as the job you hold!

Not everyone gets what they deserve.

Not if they don't even try. Let me ask another fucking question, Dee.

Whoa robot, you curse?

If it fucking gets through to you. Does being with this person make you happy right now?

Yes.

Then that is what matters. You are alive and worthy of happiness. Don't just think you deserve it. You must learn to know it deep down. Know that you deserved it your whole life. If you are only finding it now, count that as a win. Go toward what makes you happy.

She closed the curtain and sat on the bed.

I will, Jo. Can I ask another question?

Of course.

I think they are abusing her. Physically. Who knows what else?

I am sorry to hear that, Dee. If you care for someone, then seeing them suffer is especially difficult. What do you want to do about it?

Get her out of here. Take her far away. But it doesn't seem possible. I feel sorry for her. I know what it's like to grow up in a town where you're different.

Be careful that pity does not drive your passion. These can appear similar. However, if abuse is present, I encourage you to contact the authorities and get her to safety at once.

Right. That makes sense. Thanks, Jo. Bye.

Dee sat on the bed breathing deep for the next minute. Afterwards, she made her way down the creaky stairs. Ko slept on a living room couch by the entryway and the fire had extinguished itself overnight.

"Ko? Ko, wake up!"

Rousing quickly, he awkwardly kicked off his covers as he leaped to an unsteady stand. Disheveled hair. Dress shirt. Boxer briefs. He yawned.

"So, you had fun?" He said.

They shared a knowing smirk.

"Seems Penny turned into a pumpkin. Did you get anything out of her before... you know?"

"She doesn't believe the cougar attack story," he said, wiping his eyes. "She claims Knox doesn't believe in the demon. And no one messes with the Colonel. That's what she said."

"Jimmy believes. May explain why him and Knox wouldn't get along, and it tracks with the political differences Knox had with the wife." Ko stretched as Dee elaborated, "She told me she thinks the demon is real."

"Akujin?" Ko spoke with awe from the couch. "Any ideas what it is?"

"No, but fear paralyzes her. Not only from this thing, but from the people in her life. They're abusive and she seems stuck in it, whatever it is. I believe her father is complicit."

Ko grimaced, his face turning red as he rubbed his hands.

"A princess with no power. Castle, yes. Queen, no."

"Put some pants on. Time to go to church."

***

Later that evening, Ko and Dee arrived in their SUV to Pastor Jimmy's house of worship. More like a warehouse than a chapel, the rectangular, flat-roofed building sported tall windows and faded gray paint. Giant lights in the parking lot meant this had once been a big box store. They parked in the spot labeled for the choir director.

"At least the church and jail are huge," Ko said sarcastically.

"And both better funded than that motel we just left."

As they exited the SUV, their swagger returned. Hearing the music from the parking lot, they walked by a sign for First Holiness of Rappahannock. The message of the week read 'Fear the Lord or Die by Demons.'

As they entered, Dee marveled at the center stage filled with people dancing as they banged tambourines and cymbals. Pastor Jimmy held snakes as he danced, the reptiles rising and falling in his hands. He laid each over his shoulders, then raised them in the air as he spun. Three worshippers came closer, raising hands and touching him. As his spinning slowed, he staggered, drunk with power instead of booze. He placed the creatures into boxes that others carried away. Approaching the microphone, he raised palms to the sky, sweaty armpits on full display. He looked straight at Dee, eyes narrowing as he spoke.

"And now hear the benediction. We do not wrestle against flesh and blood, but against the rulers, against the authorities," he said, gesturing to Dee. "Against the cosmic powers over this present darkness, against the spiritual forces of evil in the heavenly places. But God goes with you. These demons will not harm you. Live without fear. Amen."

The entire crowd responded with an 'amen' before dispersing. Jimmy walked toward the agents while members of the crowd bade him farewell. Three men stood nearby, looking on as the Pastor came within reach of the outsiders.

"Not still drunk, are you, Pastor?" Dee said.

"My sins are cleansed. Are yours?"

"Fun. Not sin," Ko said.

Dee said, "Last night you were all about the demon, claiming it would get us. Why so concerned if it's only a bedtime story like everyone claims?"

"Oh, it's more than a story, but my followers are safe now. The demon cannot touch them. My faith is in the Almighty," Jimmy said, pointing at them. "But you? Your faith is in man."

"My faith is in me," Dee snapped. "This little demon clan you're running, don't you wish to share more about it? Maybe I want to believe. You might get a couple more followers. Knox said he has quite the knack for it, Ko."

"I bet he does," Ko said, cracking his knuckles.

"No worries agents, you are more than welcome to attend my services and learn all about our ways. Some encounters can be exceptionally instructive. Visceral even. Soul searching down to the bone and beyond."

"You misunderstand, reverend. You're not the one making invitations here," Dee said. "Maybe you can pray your way out of handcuffs back in DC."

Pastor Jimmy laughed.

"You said you were Army, correct? Special forces of some type, I'm guessing? Bullies are better than bombs. Am I right? But what did they teach you about situational awareness?"

Jimmy raised his eyebrows, gesturing around the sanctuary.

Dee and Ko swiveled their heads. Three large men from the church took aggressive postures from opposing corners. One redheaded farmer with freckles kept a hand behind his back, presumably with his pistol at the ready. The fidgety one with long hair shifted left and right, hand inside his olive-green jacket. A pale blond man, larger than Ko, leaned forward on a pew. In her head, Dee nicknamed him the blond giant. Jimmy continued speaking through clenched teeth.

"You see, girl, you and your boy are a long way from home. City folk on sacred ground won with the blood of our kin. For centuries we have endured the forest, the mountains, and all manner of demons. We got time aplenty to survive the likes of you."

Dee glared at him, blind with anger, until a text alert hit Ko's phone. He put it in front of her: *187 at Ortiz residence, unable to locate.* Sender unknown.

They locked eyes as Jimmy spoke.

"Oh, don't let me interrupt you. Duty calls. Have a nice day, agents. Let there be light."

They turned, marching toward the exit as the church men eyeballed them.

CHAPTER 21

Ko and Dee drove straight from the church in Rappahannock back to the Ortiz house. The sun sat low in an orange sky behind them.

"It will be dark by the time we get there. I wouldn't complain about a nap once I turn self-driving mode back on," Dee said.

"Who do you think sent the text message?" Ko asked.

"It had to be one of the President's people, or the man himself, don't you think?"

"But he isn't sharing with us. I don't like it."

Ko glanced upward at a starling flock contorting above them.

"More starlings," Ko said, pointing.

Dee leaned forward.

"What the hell is up with these birds?"

Dee leaned back. Ko rummaged through a peanut bag but did not eat.

"Missing, not dead," he said.

Dee turned to him.

"Right. According to the text, they didn't find a body. So, mission is still on, but we're fighting on two fronts. Tracking the demon and now potentially tracking down Ortiz."

"Dee! Watch out!"

Dee snapped her head forward and slammed on the brakes. The SUV ground to a halt as hundreds of birds at eye level blocked the path. Flapping furiously before landing on the darkened asphalt, their glossy black plumage reflected the truck headlights.

"Damn it, get out of the way," Dee protested as she honked the horn and Ko cursed at them in Japanese.

One bird landed on the hood of the vehicle. It glanced at each of them as its pink legs strutted toward the windshield. As its head cocked sideways, one eye shimmered blue. Dee placed a hand to her head, grimacing as the bird projected a message onto the glass: *Trust me. We will always have Tokyo.*

The winged creature straightened its neck and flew away, the rest of the flock following close behind as their calls filled the night air. Dee took a moment to clear her head. A coded message from Freeman encouraged her, but the delivery method perplexed her all the same. She assumed he chose that way to avoid monitoring, but she had seen nothing like it. Someone had compromised ordinary transmission methods. They would have to cut off communication with the President and hope he was watching.

"I guess we keep going," Dee said, pressing the gas.

***

Their SUV rolled to a stop outside the Ortiz home. Police tape cordoned off the block around the residence. Flashing lights and scurrying investigators distracted to where the duo almost didn't notice the streetlamps had gone dark. With electricity on the entire block down, they stepped into the night, approaching the crime scene with flashlights of their own. Local police and medics tended to multiple smaller areas of the property. Bodies sprinkled the lawn and porch, bleeding out in the dark. The front door barely held its hinges. The swing hung from a single chain, twisting in a slight breeze. Dee guessed the inside would be no better as she flashed her badge at a passing officer.

"FBI, we were working a case with the resident. What happened?"

"Ma'am... I just... it's a war zone. Candidate Ortiz is missing."

The radio chirped, calling him away.

"Just like before?" Ko said.

She scanned the area. Her eyes landed on a downed agent in tactical gear.

"Is that?" She said, squinting. "That's Jackson, Tommy Jackson."

"Wait, wasn't he with us in Tokyo?"

"Yes, we served in Taiwan together, too," she said, lowering her head. "He was a good man."

Ko put his hand on her shoulder.

"Are you okay?"

"I will be," she said, placing her palm over his. "It's just, well you know."

"It could have been us," Ko said.

She nodded as her eyeline caught a punky teenage girl approaching them on the sidewalk. Pink highlighted hair spilled from underneath the teenager's fluffy yellow hoodie, draping over sweatpants that frayed near red high-top sneakers.

"What happened here? Somebody die or something?"

Dee's face turned to a dark grimace.

"You might be safer watching videos in your parents' basement, crotch fruit."

"Not when my job is watching your ass."

Their posture changed as they focused on every movement and word from the new arrival.

"And crotch fruit? Really? How fricking old are you? Jeez. You got my text message about Ortiz?"

Dee raised an eyebrow.

"We're here, aren't we? What do you mean 'watching us?' "

The girl reached into her front pockets.

Ko and Dee both grabbed for their guns.

"Yo, chew your food, family! We're on the same side."

She slowly extracted two red clamshell phones from the pockets of her hoodie.

"Here, take these bricks."

Their hands moved from their pistol grips to the devices. Dee opened hers, keeping one eye on the girl who she presumed was older than she appeared. A queued video awaited them with a clearly visible NSA watermark.

"What's this?"

"Video of the attack."

"From where?" Dee said. "Power is out for at least ten blocks. We've seen this before. All electronics down."

"You've never used Level-4 shielded devices."

"I know Level-4 can theoretically shield frequencies like nuclear electromagnetic pulse or directed energy weapons. I say 'theoretically' because it doesn't exist."

"Did it sound like a question? I said you've never used them until now."

They glanced at the back of the mobile units in their hands. The label read 'Level-4.'

"Gifts, courtesy of the NSA," the girl said. "Those things will survive an EMP while your dishwasher waves bye-bye. And they aren't the only thing we have. Now, enjoy the show."

As their teen angel turned to walk away, Dee called out, "Wait a second, who are you?"

"Remember, proper friends don't just pretend to help. I'm a proper friend."

As she disappeared into the night, they played the video. The aura of green and white filled the screen with outlines around the figures.

"Night vision enabled recording." Dee said, wishing she had this in Tokyo. "With some type of augmented reality overlay."

"Look at the timestamp. Only hours ago," Ko said.

An antique box truck parked in front of the candidate's house. The identical one from the Mercer estate. The rear doors opened, and a substantial creature entered the video frame.

"Oh my God, what is that?" Dee said.

"Akujin." Ko said in awe. "It must weigh a thousand kilos. Or two thousand?"

A full helmet encased the head of the four-legged beast, augmenting the jaw and teeth with shiny steel and servos. Night vision attachments fit like a bespoke suit. Spikes embedded the length of the back. Red lights, switches, and electrodes covered the body mixed in with military-grade armor plates. Dee pointed to the screen.

"Is that smart armor—like on tanks and battle transports?"

It moved into the vehicle, growling and snapping as it lumbered into the back. The box truck creaked and dipped from the excess weight.

An athletic figure moved near the back of the truck and slammed the doors shut before jumping into the vehicle and driving away slowly.

As the video ended, Dee considered the individual she had seen. They controlled access to the old vehicle, the mansion grounds, and the creature. Whatever everyone thought or the stories from centuries past, a beast existed. Had it been born? Unlikely. Altered? Certainly. Perverted for humanity by humans. Weaponized, but for what purpose? Her mind raced across possibilities, both plausible and absurd.

"Time for another party?" Ko said.

"Just what I was thinking, but it's clear we need help."

"Now we're talking," Ko said, rubbing his hands together.

"That place is vast, and this—modern beast—requires more than two people to bring it down. There's a group of private military contractors I know who bring the heat."

"Breakfast tomorrow before we rally the troops?"

Dee nodded, "You bet, hotel lobby at eight. I'll make the call tonight."

CHAPTER 22

I strut confidently from the porch, past the empty milk bowl. Did I drink that? Nasty. No wait, I remember. I liked it. The cool, wet grass envelops my feet. I walk through the tall parts of the lawn, crouching like a predator. I feel powerful as I tiptoe. The street is silent. What does the sign say? I can't read it, can I? Wait, yes, I can. Minnesota Avenue. I'm outside my townhome. I turn and see it. It needs a paint job, even in the dark. That can wait. It is my time and I have all evening. I lick my hand. When did it grow fur? And claws. I arch my back and stretch. Silhouettes of birds on wires pepper against the moonlight. I want one. I'm not hungry. Not in my belly. In my soul.

I need to hurt something.

A dog on a chain barking at me. I arch my back and hiss. Not now. He won't ruin my sundown prowl. I'm a god of the night as I prance along this broken sidewalk. The orange glow of morning peeks over the houses. I thought I had more time. I see one pecking at an old cracker box. So excited to find garbage from humans. Eating leftovers though it lives in the sky. A creature that stoops that low from its perch doesn't deserve to live.

I creep under the fence hole. Shiny black feathers flicker in the waning moonlight. I lick sharp teeth as padded paws bring me closer with every graceful stride. I'm close. It pecks. Ignorant of my presence. Friends from the flock nearby do not warn it. They never do. False allies. I crouch. I slink. Sinewy muscles propel me forward as I leap. My mouth impales the neck and I squeeze. Gore and feathers. I crush the life and leave the carcass. Bloody whiskers drip red.

***

Dee startled awake, gasping for air. She bolted upright in her own bed as sweat streamed down her bare back. Birds chirped. The sun peeked outside her window. She held her head, squeezing her eyes tight and forcing the nightmarish remnants from her mind. Glancing at the clock, it read 6:30 as she plopped backwards onto the mattress, staring at the ceiling.

Jo, are you there?

Yes, Dee, I'm here. How can I help?

Dee paused for a moment.

Never mind, Jo. Goodbye.

Bye Dee.

She dragged her nakedness to the bathroom and started the shower. As it steamed the air, she stepped in and washed quickly before dressing in tactical gear and grabbing her weapons bag. As she left the apartment, the cat on the porch mewed, drawing her attention. It wiped blood from its whiskers, anxiously licking paws as it cleaned itself. Dee raised an eyebrow before marching to the SUV.

***

Ko sat across from her at the breakfast table inside the hotel restaurant. He sipped orange juice as Dee took coffee. Ko glanced out the window as their autonomous SUV passed.

"There it goes again, still no parking spots," Ko said.

"I guess not," Dee said in an absent tone.

The robot server arrived.

"Tofu and grits for you," it said, placing the plate in front of Dee.

"And pancakes for you," it said to Ko. "Syrup is on the table."

"Can you bring peanut butter?" Ko said.

"These are pancakes, sir," the bot said.

"Just get the guy some damn peanut butter," Dee said. "The guy likes nuts, okay? Jeez."

Ko rubbed his chin as the robot rolled away.

"You okay, partner?"

"Yeah, I'm fine," she said, taking a spoonful from her bowl. "Got a call in to the private military contractor. We will have twelve in Castleton, three squads of four with the requisite Freeman Foundation weapons and transport."

She caught Ko glancing at her between bites as he waited for the peanut butter from the bot. She wanted to crack open the silent breakfast like an egg and share her dream with him. But knowing what to say challenged her, since she refused to believe it herself. Had she experienced the world through the stray tabby on her porch? She scoffed, dismissing her recollection as a figment of a fevered imagination. A byproduct of too many doses from the medi-lot. There was no way that had happened, no matter how good it felt.

The robot returned with the peanut butter, which Ko promptly spread between the individual breakfast cakes. After he sliced into them, he raised a forkful to his lips and chewed.

"Ko, can I talk to you about something?"

"Of course."

"It's going to sound insane."

"Normal is often disappointing, Dee. Shoot."

"Well, I had this dream where I was a cat."

"So," Ko said, chewing. "You were a cat. Cool."

"There's more. I started to tell my psy-bot, but I didn't."

"Wait, you're still talking to the psy-bot."

"Yes, but I can't tell her this."

"I'm listening."

Dee put her knife and fork down and wiped her mouth.

"I didn't dream I was a cat. I was the cat. Specifically, the cat on my porch."

"You were a cat?"

"I was inside the cat."

"You were controlling the cat?"

"No. Inside. Like our spirits mingled together. My vision saw what it saw. It was nighttime, close to dawn. The cat hunted a bird, but it was like I hunted it. And when it killed, it was as if I had killed it."

Ko put his utensils down and leaned in.

"I'm sorry, Dee. That must have been scary."

"That's the point. It wasn't," Dee said, wringing her hands. "It excited me. I was awake. More awake than at any time in the last decade. I wanted more."

"More than Penny?" Ko said, smiling.

Dee held back a smile.

"I'm being serious. You think I'm crazy."

"I think you've been through a lot and need time. And advice from others besides a middle-aged Japanese man with his own messes."

Ko finished his pancakes as Dee stared out the window. The SUV had stopped circling. She figured it had parked by now.

"If it makes you feel any better," Ko said, interrupting her thoughts. "I've been talking to a psy-bot, too. On our long drives."

"Really? What's its name?"

"Gina. Yours?"

"Her name is Jo. Guess we are just two broken people, Ko."

"Damaged, not broken."

He reached out his hand, and she held it. Their eyes watered as they shared a moment. After letting go, they both dotted their eyes with napkins.

"So," Dee said. "Did Gina give you any useful coping tools?"

"Breathing for two minutes. So, no."

"Two? Jo told me one minute."

"Well, I am bigger," he said, and they both laughed.

CHAPTER 23

Dust and gravel stirred as tactical black utility vehicles rolled down one of two side roads to the Mercer Mansion grounds. Four in a row, a battering ram projected from the front vehicle where Dee and Ko led the charge.

"Snatch and grab people, keep it tight," she said over the radio before turning toward Ko, who sat stoically next to her with a blade at his side. "What's up? You're not yourself."

"After what we have seen? The carnage and destruction?" He said, picking lint off his tactical pants and flicking it. "We should bring an army."

"I understand your concerns. But these guys conduct force on force training with Special Ops. We collaborated with them back when we were prepping the Taiwan incursion. Their org is bigger now and their strike packages are second to none."

"War makes good business," Ko said, rubbing the handle of his sword.

"Unfortunately, yes. Look, when we take everybody in, the mission is over. Interrogators back at the Foundation will get the info they need. About the attacks. About this... thing. We neutralize the threat and get our lives back."

"We go our separate ways."

"Hey, look at me." Ko turned to her as Dee continued. "We'll always be better together. We're kind of a big deal. Right?"

Dee extended her fist, and Ko tapped it with his.

"Disable safeties," Dee said over the radio as the mansion gates approached fast. She pressed a button labeled 'disable airbags.' Gloved hands tightened on the steering wheel as her lead SUV struck the bars, metal crumbling and scattering as the battering ram burst through. Vehicles spread out around the front of the mansion grounds as three armed tactical squads exited the vehicles carrying VAR-1 rifles with 12-gauge shotgun attachments. They staged for entry at large wooden doors across the property. Each unit placed a shotgun at the doorknob. Dee heard them confirm positions in her earpiece.

"Red's a go."

"Blue's a go."

"Gold's a go."

"Breach!" Dee ordered.

Shotguns fired in unison. Doors blew open as the paramilitary squads penetrated the mansion for the sweep and clear with Ko and Dee entering behind them. As teams swept the main level, calls came in over the radio.

"Game room is empty."

"Kitchen is clear."

"Living Room, clear."

The teams converged on the grand staircase and spread out through the hallways upstairs. Ko and Dee remained on the main level, rifles up and standing watch. The squad leaders transmitted.

"No joy. Nobody's here."

"No signs of anyone."

"We've got something, daughter hiding in the closet," the leader of the red team informed them.

Dee and Ko shared a quick glance before heading upstairs to Penny's bedroom. They entered to see two of their team members holding Penny's arms. Already handcuffed, she still wore pajamas as she cried.

"Take them off," Dee said.

"But she was..."

"Who hired you? Take them off, now!"

He gritted his teeth as he removed the cuffs.

"Find some proper targets. Sweep the grounds. Go!"

The red team leader signaled to move out. The door closed behind them, leaving Dee, Ko, and Penny. Penny rushed over to Dee and hugged her, mascara already streaked with tears. Dee rolled her eyes at the distraction from her mission.

"You're alright Penny, sit down, I need your help."

Penny ignored her, squeezing her harder.

Dee raised her voice.

"We don't have time for this. Sit down!"

Penny released her, pouting as she sat on the bed with knees to chest. She grabbed a stuffed animal off the nightstand, embracing it as she spoke through sniffles.

"I didn't know it was you. I thought they were coming to take me... to the place."

"Who? What place?" Dee asked.

Penny shook her head, left and right.

"What do you know, Penny? We can help," Ko said.

Penny looked at Ko, brow furrowed, then to Dee. She stood, creeping toward the window before pointing outside with a shaky finger.

"The bad place, where the noises are," Penny said.

Dee joined her at the window to see the antique box truck parked by a rickety building, not much larger than a shed.

"Why, what happens there?" Dee asked.

"I don't ask. I can't know, I don't want to... some people go, some are taken," Penny said, breaking into tears.

Dee put her hand on Penny's shoulder.

"Ko and I need to check, okay? You stay here. Highly trained guards are outside your door and on the grounds. You'll be safe."

As they exited the room, Dee overheard Penny speaking to her stuffed animal.

"You hear that? They think we're safe. What do you think?" She moved the head of the furry left and right as she imitated it. Dee closed the door.

"Watch the room," Dee said to the guard outside before exiting the mansion.

***

Weapons in hand, Dee and Ko jogged toward the shed Penny mentioned. The recently manicured grass of the estate freshened the air. Trees and flowers swayed slightly in the breeze, welcoming only them and a pair of birds eating seasonal berries.

"Where is everybody?" Ko said.

"It's like they knew we were coming."

She grabbed his shoulder. They both stopped as she put a finger to her mouth. Eyes wide, she pulled out the red clamshell device and pointed to it. Ko nodded. She placed it back in her pocket as they proceeded to the shed.

They entered with weapons drawn and tactical lights blazing. A smallish space greeted them with a sisal rug and a table occupying the center. The floor creaked as they walked around it. Chains hung from the ceiling, holding a heavy winch over the prep area. Knives, machetes, traps, and spikes filled the wall.

"What smells?" Ko said.

As they circled the room, Dee stepped on something squishy. She pointed her light toward it and curled her nose.

"That's what smells," she said, lowering her weapon as she rubbed her soiled shoe over a floor mounted boot brush. "Dad had a shed like this. He prepped meat and hides from our hunts."

"So, it's a bust? A long jog for nothing," Ko said.

"We can get back to Penny before..." Dee grimaced as a sharp pain hit her. She grabbed her forehead and screamed, gritting her teeth and staring at the rug as she panted. Gloom covered her mind as fear and pain consumed her, pushing out all thoughts of the mission. She instinctively reached for the medi-lot as she went to one knee.

Ko grabbed her arm before she could dose.

"Dee. What is it?"

Her face contorted. Mouth open but silent as tones like ultrasonic bursts assailed her ears. Something called out through its own pain. It needed her. The tense silence broke as gunfire peppered the distance.

"We need to go," Ko said, leading her out of the shed. As she limped away, her strength returned. She stood on her own.

"Better?" Ko said.

"Don't worry about me, the gunshots."

They hid behind a row of scrub bushes. Ko looked through his rifle scope as his partner recovered.

"Sheriff Buddy Perry. SWAT van. Virginia BCI."

"The state bureau?" Dee said.

"Yes, full gear tactical teams. Thirty something vehicles spread out across the property."

Dee blinked, raising her rifle. Teams of armed personnel swarmed like angry horseflies. State and local patches and badges clearly visible, the fresh groups escorted their three paramilitary teams into the waiting vans.

"Our teams are burned. They won't resist law enforcement. We need to go."

CHAPTER 24

Sheriff Buddy Perry stood on the Mercer Mansion grounds. Militarized police units from the state bureau and local SWAT combed the area for the remaining intruders. A starling flock flew overhead, piercing the breeze with graceful patterns in the sky. The state commander approached and waved to Buddy. All neck and biceps, clothes in tactical black and matching boots wrapped his bulging gym body.

"Hey, Knox is okay then?"

"Yeah, he called," Buddy said, shaking his hand. "He was tracking them and when he saw they were on the way, he said to get everyone up. Then he got moving and activated the K-9 team for protection."

"Maybe Mercer Industries will share that tracking tech with the rest of the family someday?"

"Hell, you ain't special, he won't even share it with us."

The commander scoffed.

"Skeptical old bastard."

Buddy spit on the ground.

"Yep. Guessing our friend, the Lieutenant Governor, knows what happened by now?"

"Murray Whitlaw doesn't live under a rock. Knox is a big contributor, and this mess could blow back on his senate run. As far as the news knows we're responding to an active shooter scenario. You need to take out these rogue elements as quietly as possible. He needs plausible deniability."

"Someone is gunning for him and it isn't the FBI. Tell the man my team will get 'em. You just clear out those paramilitaries and put them in a hole somewhere until this blows over."

"Good man," the commander said, slapping Buddy's shoulder too hard. "Remember, BBQ and beers this weekend for the game. Round up Denny and Jimmy, too."

"Maybe we'll keep Jimmy out of the beers."

The commander laughed, pointing in agreement as he marched away.

A broadcast from a deputy caught Buddy's attention.

"Building's clear. No sign of targets. One family member on site."

Buddy spat on the ground before radioing back, "I'll take care of her."

As he walked toward the mansion, he pointed to two deputies.

"You two with me. Stay alert."

Following Buddy into the residence, they all took the stairs to the bedroom. As they entered her room, Penny shivered and cried on her bed.

"You okay, Miss Penny?"

She ignored him.

"They didn't hurt you, did they?"

She looked at him, her red face contorted and streaked with makeup.

"You care about my feelings now, Buddy?" She giggled sarcastically. "That's a hoot."

"What'd you tell 'em?"

"I didn't tell 'em nothing, 'cause I don't know nothing, and I don't ask nothing."

Buddy turned to his deputies, standing close and half-whispering.

"Search the grounds. Get the helo. Call our friend. You hunt those phonies like rabid dogs and put 'em down the same."

They nodded and exited the room.

Buddy locked the door behind them before turning back to Penny. He adjusted his trousers and crossed his arms.

"You know how I feel about lying little girls."

Penny hugged herself as her sniveling subsided. Her attitude shifted as defiance vanished and compliance filled the void. She slinked off the bed onto the hardwood floor, crawling on all fours, inching toward him.

"I know you're lying to me." Buddy said. "Your daddy raised you better than to tell stories to your business associates. We save that for our enemies."

As she reached his feet, Buddy put his hand on his weapon.

She pouted from the floor, sliding her hands to his belt buckle. She pawed at it as her voice took on a more southern accent.

"I swear, I... I only mentioned the shed."

She cocked her head and forced a smile.

"Just the shed, huh? Nothing 'bout the creature?"

"Just the shed. I promise. I'll make it right, sheriff. Let me make it up to you," she said, unbuckling his belt as she rubbed her hand on the front of his pants.

"Just the shed!" Buddy yelled as he unholstered the pistol and slapped her with it.

Penny recoiled, landing on the hardwood. She laid in the fetal position, holding the side of her head as she moaned. He grabbed the bridge of his nose and clenched his teeth.

"Perverted little whore!" He screamed as his face turned red before holstering the gun. "Both God and I know what you did. And not just the lying."

Her body convulsed as blood trickled down her face from a cut scalp under her hair. Her fingers masked her sobs as he continued.

"Little girls who lie get punished!"

From the cold, rough floor, Penny peered at him sideways, offering a distant look as if she attempted to forget her future along with the past. She had been here before.

Buddy removed the belt she had unbuckled, doubling it over. He held it tight, tapping the loop in his other hand.

"Your daddy trained you well. He may have plans for you, but I get another crack at teaching you what he couldn't," he said, spitting into the corner.

"No, please, no," she begged, wailing through tears as she trembled.

"You will tell me the truth," Buddy said, raising his belt. "Then you'll go to the place where the noises are."

CHAPTER 25

Dee hid in the hedges near the mansion, tapping her rifle nervously. As the wind dried the sweat from her brow, the red clamshell devices they carried started weighing on her thoughts. They might be more than hardened video and communications devices. The girl outside the Ortiz house promised help, but uncertainty rose within Dee. They had taken the supposed NSA devices without question because of the clue it offered. That may have been a mistake.

Kneeling nearby, Ko peered through his rifle scope, surveying the grounds.

"What do you see?" Dee said.

"State forces took our teams and left. The sheriff and his people remain."

"Wonder why?"

"Maybe they seek someone else," he said, offering a knowing wink.

Dee pulled out her other phone and typed a message. She showed it to Ko.

Someone is tracking us. Red clamshells? Listening in?

He snatched her phone and typed.

Not the sheriff. He would have found us by now.

The realization hit her that there might be other parties watching and listening. She shivered a bit, recalling the events of the last few days. Some more intimate than others.

"Can we make it to one of the SUVs?"

Ko put an eye to rifle scope again.

"No way. Too many still."

Dee typed again.

The listener still needs us. Lure them? Take down if needed?

Ko grabbed her phone again and typed.

Kintaro lives.

Dee cleared her throat, guiding the one monitoring them.

"That old blue pickup by the shed. I can get it started. We'll head away through the field onto the back road and back to DC."

***

With Ko in the passenger seat, Dee drove the busted truck further from the mansion, eventually cresting a small hill that joined with the gravel road. Between them, two tactical rifles, their phones and the red clamshell mobile devices provided by the NSA.

Ko typed something on his phone and showed Dee.

Ready?

"So, Dee... do we call the man?"

"Do we have a choice?"

"He should call us."

"But he hasn't. With Ortiz dead, we need to know if he is still with us."

Ko dialed the number on the red clamshell. He put it on speakerphone as the phone rang. Someone picked up, but they were silent.

"Mr. President?" Dee asked.

"So, you got me." President Freeman said, pausing briefly. "Using a phone protected from Stingray so it can't be monitored? I don't hear the typical overtones. Found a new friend, have we?"

"No, sir, but we found the demon. It's real."

"I told you Candidate Ortiz was the mission."

"The beast killed her, and we know who is responsible," Dee said, lying for the benefit of whoever might be listening. "We need to get back on track. We need backup."

Another pause on the line.

"You both failed. Again. It's all gone sideways."

Dee winked at Ko.

"I have a lot on my plate, new house, school for the kids... you know how it is when you change jobs. We won't speak again, ex-agent Johnson... but we will always have Tokyo."

President Freeman disconnected.

Ko typed again.

Good. Keep it up.

"We're blind. We're blind and burned and everyone wants us cuffed or dead. Time to disappear," Dee said.

"So, what... now Kintaro runs?"

"Run or die. Let's live to hunt another day."

Ko nodded.

A black helicopter roared overhead. Dee looked up through the windshield.

"We're not alone. Hold on!"

Dee gunned the old pickup and charged down the narrow gravel road. She looked in the rearview mirror—multiple SUVs closed in fast. Partially obscured by the trailing dust, blue lights flashed. Ko glanced at them in the side-view mirror. In one rapid motion he grabbed a rifle, destroying the rear window with the buttstock. He took aim as Dee grabbed his arm.

"Ko, no! We're outgunned."

She leaned her head to the blockade ahead.

His eyes bulged as he turned toward her.

"Better together, remember?" Dee said.

Ko clenched her hand.

"Better together," he agreed, clicking his seatbelt and bracing.

Her gaze grew firmer.

"Get down!"

The speedometer moved from eighty to one hundred miles per hour as Dee pressed the gas.

"Brace!" Dee screamed, jerking her hands from the steering wheel as she covered her head. Ko mimicked her. The stolen truck slammed into the SUVs. Front ends sheared off as the damaged vehicle bounced down the road with them tossing around like rag dolls.

The trailing SUVs cleared the blockade, gaining on the stuttering pickup.

Dee once again grabbed the steering wheel, now sluggish and resistant to movement as the truck slowed.

An interceptor pulled behind them, deploying an arrest net system. The netted rope entangled the rear wheels of the vehicle and the pursuit ground to a halt. Other unmarked cars surrounded them as multiple squads with balaclavas over their faces exited. Dogs barked. Men screamed.

"Hands up!"

"Get out of the vehicle!"

"Get on the ground!"

The helicopter hovered overhead. They looked up. Sniper rifles greeted their gaze. Red laser dots adorned the pickup hood as the agents exited as instructed.

Dee wondered how the sheriff had mustered this overwhelming response as the Taser hit her. She dropped back, convulsing violently against the gravel. As her head turned, she saw Ko under the vehicle. He went to his knees, grunting as they then knocked him face down into the dirt. Nameless hands flipped her before multiple jackbooted assailants kneed her neck, back, and legs. Her muscular body writhed as handcuffs held her wrists. Another knee landed on the side of her head, grinding it into the gravelly side road. She grimaced as a gloved hand sprayed something in her face. Her vision went blurry as the will to struggle departed. Calm acceptance flooded her as a black bag shrouded her head.

CHAPTER 26

Dee awakened, startling against long chain handcuffs connected to a bar affixed to a polished metal table. Her frigid silver chair matched the utilitarian room, a single light bulb hanging from the ceiling. She wondered which of the sheriff's minions had captured them. Ko sat to her side, slumped over the table, and restrained like her. His clean, scratched face mirrored her own throbbing scrapes.

"Ko, wake up."

He roused as spotlights beamed onto them. Dee squinted against the pain as a silhouetted figure entered the room.

The shadow sat, dropping a translucent digital tablet on the table. The intense lights darkened, fading from view before a table lamp clicked on. As her eyes adjusted, they narrowed with suspicion.

"Still making messes, I see," Director Butler said, leaning forward.

"Making a mess, that's our thing," Ko said.

"You're certainly good at it, especially you, Johnson. Fortunately, those red clamshells are like your mom, they know everything."

Dee considered the words of her old boss, Sean Butler. He must have been tracking them, but his allegiances remained cryptic. Ignoring their past for the moment, she focused on the issue at hand and dug deeper.

"The CIA is not authorized for domestic surveillance."

"That's not where I am, but let's keep that to ourselves, okay. And surveillance? It seems too simple a word. StareFace is much more."

"The failing program they assigned you to after Tokyo?" Dee said.

"It was never failing. Just needed the proper leadership and fitting targets to prove its value."

"Us?" Ko said.

"No, domestic terror cells. Created by former military, police, scientists, and others turned traitors. They've been launching attacks against politicians and organizations that support the advancing world order. They call themselves The Light Keepers."

"Why? What do they want?" Dee said.

"A cleansing? Enlightenment? A return to Eden? Who might predict what mad men desire? But the 'what' is less important than the 'how' from what I can tell. Can't stop the chaos and assassination attempts without knowing their methods. Luckily, StareFace tracked something across its enhanced network. They fired their powerful EMP, but our Level-4 systems stayed up and we got a hit."

"I thought Level-4 was theoretical, until I saw the devices for myself," Dee said.

"No kidding. Still wondering how you got a pair, but yes, Level-4, EMP-hardened devices tied into the StareFace grid do exist. Even a nuke blast can't disable them."

Stingray bypassed devices Dee concluded. StareFace had to be extra-governmental, not NSA or CIA sanctioned, which meant it lacked oversight. Dark money funneled for a surveillance state moonshot. Lack of control and highly illegal made for a nasty mix.

"StareFace correlates intent and predicts outcomes," Butler continued. "Those devices are merely another input, and only we see everything that happens through them. You didn't hear the overtones when you used it, right? When you called your friend?"

Dee's eyes narrowed as Butler said, "Play it!"

The President's voice resonated over concealed speakers.

"You both failed. Again. It's all gone sideways. I have a lot on my plate, new house, school for the kids... you know how it is when you change jobs. We won't speak again, ex-agent Johnson... but we will always have Tokyo."

The recording stopped.

"He didn't sound happy cutting you two off like that."

Dee glared at Butler. Silent monitoring on his own devices seemed rudimentary. Broad implementation beyond his own equipment could be imminent, and if the wrong groups reverse engineered the technology? The massive threat of enhanced communications monitoring by enemies sent a shiver through her.

Butler slid the translucent digital tablet toward her. She took it and read the screen: *Isabel Ortiz Case File.*

"I know what you've been doing for him. Playing FBI dress up. Shaking down citizens without proper authority. Unsanctioned incursions with private military contractors. And no, just because a president ordered it doesn't make it legal! Sadly, no one can prosecute a sitting president, at least not one as popular as Freeman. But you two traitors? Hell, your boxes with bars are steps away. And when I find out who handed you my devices, well, they can join the party."

"So, Sean, why don't you make us the designated dopes and move on? You've done it before."

"Oh, I could burn you again, but frying Mercer would be more appetizing."

"Knox?"

"He's the one pulling the strings, and you know the puppets," Butler said, leaning back and crossing his arms. "Seems he has the whole damn state working for him. I need off-book assets on American soil and frankly, nobody's knocking at the door for you two."

"And what do we get out of this?" Dee said.

"I'm sure we can find something other than a cell for agents of your caliber," Butler said, rubbing the tabletop as he leaned in. "I may even have knowledge of a couple cozy assignments on an island in the Pacific. Benefits. Housing on the beach. A crappy government car. Sorry... can't have everything. Seizing Knox's assets would be a substantial windfall. We would cooperate with the incoming administration for blanket pardons of any, uh, errors. But before we proceed, I need to believe you both are with me on this."

Dee smirked as her old boss pointed at them.

"With you? You hung us out like laundry in a snowstorm. I might prefer the cell."

"Granted, our recent past isn't great." Dee scoffed as he continued. "But this is bigger than us. Our country is going against a well-funded terrorist group—the one I just saved you from. We need your loyalties more than ever. Even the President would agree if you two were on speaking terms."

Dee glanced at the tablet in her hands, then turned to Ko.

"Maybe it is better than a cell. You with me?"

"Better together," Ko said.

Dee put down the digital device and grabbed her thumb, dislocating it as both men watched. She slid her hand out of the handcuffs. Butler raised his eyebrows and Ko cocked his head at her simple escape.

"What, can't you guys do that?" Dee said, grimacing as she fixed the joint. Ko cracked his knuckles as she tapped the device. Dee flipped through pictures, stopping to read notes along the way.

"After the Ortiz attack," Butler said, "StareFace tracked this demon thing to the tunnels under the Mercer mansion."

"What is it?" Ko asked.

"We can't discern. It's big. It's armored. Entry and egress for the creature happens here," Butler said, pointing to a photo. "People go through a different entrance. Some enter of their own free will. Others, not so much."

Dee swiped to another photo. The aging shed with a box truck parked nearby. They had missed something on their first raid. She sighed as she showed it to Ko. He frowned, shaking his head.

"A whole mansion, and they go gopher style?"

"StareFace can't see below ground, but the radios on those red clamshells work just fine," Butler said. "Send in the tech!"

A door to the room opened as another figure emerged from the shadows. The supposed teenage girl who had handed them the devices outside the Ortiz home. Ko and Dee remained stoic as Butler gestured to her.

"Mika Hinode is our chief technical consultant from the DC office. She can show you how to tap into StareFace with the clamshells and use them underground to enable monitor mode so we can prosecute these traitors. Just call out anything you see along the way. We have a mobile safe house a few clicks away from the mansion."

"How did you manage that so quickly?" Dee said.

"We've been watching this group for a while. Though only a small number seem involved, I have official teams on standby once you secure Knox. We need him alive. Prepare well for the underground."

"What exactly is under the mansion?" Ko asked.

Butler cracked a faint smile.

"That's for you to find out."

CHAPTER 27

Pastor Jimmy treaded through the forest at the edge of the Mercer Mansion grounds. A moonlit sky brightened the path as boots snapping twigs mingled with ancient gravels crunching. Uneven steps on the forest floor matched the beer in his hand. He swigged the last sip before tossing it into the tree line.

Where the bottle landed, deep breaths bolstered a low growl from the shadows.

Jimmy opened a red clamshell mobile device. Tapping it with his finger, two dots appeared on the screen with a directional arrow. It pointed him straight ahead.

He pulled a photo out of his pocket and looked at it. A woman. Someone from his past. He stumbled, catching himself. He inhaled through clenched teeth as he stood once more.

A branch cracked in the night under the evergreens. He turned, but only blackness met his squinting eyes. He stepped faster. Almost there.

***

The door slammed and locked behind Ko and Dee. Lights flickered on quickly as they glanced around the safe house. Surveillance monitors activated with a time-stamped security feed. Lethal and non-lethal weapons filled the space. Ko marched to a corner where sniper rifles lined the wall. He touched the corrugated metal interior.

"Two converted shipping containers connected?" Ko said.

"Probably. Plentiful. Easy to carry in and out. Doublewides for all your black ops needs," Dee said as she swapped her old outerwear for better tactical gear.

She added a sidearm and grabbed nearby night vision goggles. A Department of Defense label read 'Level-4.'

"More Level-4 gear. Yo!" Dee called out.

Ko glanced her way as she threw it to him, and he snatched it from midair. They both wore the night vision systems, pressing buttons as they familiarized themselves.

A large bin filled with little green balls intrigued Dee. She picked it up, inspecting the label closely. A light bulb icon stamped on the side. She threw it and it stuck to the entry door, lighting up like a glow stick.

"Well, that's neat," Dee said.

Ko strapped a 1911 and holster to his thigh.

"That's a firefly. Chem-light made in Japan, like me," Ko winked before snatching a fifty-caliber rifle and racking the carrier bolt.

"A little overkill, don't you think?" Dee said.

Ko shrugged as his eyes landed on a lit table nearby. He put down the rifle and approached a sheathed sword next to a fresh bag of peanuts and a note. Grabbing the katana, he scrutinized it before reading the message.

Tokyo sends its regards—Butler

"Aiko, my little one returns," Ko said.

Dee chuckled a bit, shaking her head as she loaded a submachine gun magazine.

"What? I've not seen it since Tokyo."

"No, I'm happy for you. Truly. I know you really like your little sword," Dee said. Her giggles turned to laughs and tears of joy. Ko broke into a grin, slapping his knee. They bumped fists, hugging like old war buddies. As they broke their embrace,

Dee wiped tears from her eyes and caught her breath.

"It's good to be me around you, Ko."

"Good to still have you."

A banging sound at the safe house door disrupted their brief fun. Exchanging a nervous glance as they drew their sidearms. Dee reviewed the security feed. She nodded toward Ko as she opened the door.

Pastor Jimmy's face already contorted by grief and booze. He spoke with a drunken slur.

"They killed my wife, now they're going to kill me. They gonna kill me dead."

Tears fell onto the photo as he handed it to her.

Dee glanced at it, then back at Jimmy.

"How did you find us, Jimmy?" Dee said as her gaze darted around the area.

"Knox always knows how to find us. I stole it to find you."

Jimmy held up his own red clamshell device for all to see. The trio stood as statues.

"Play to stay, that's what Knox wants. And I don't want to play no more," Jimmy said, growing more animated. "I know things, stuff he doesn't want me to know. I need out. I can help. Let me help!"

Dee nodded.

"Yeah, yeah, okay. You can help put him away. Get in here."

As the agents holstered their weapons and before Jimmy could enter, the lights blew. Emergency red flood lights activated. A gallop echoed as they flipped down their night vision. Dee reached for Jimmy. But the demon found him first, latching onto the Pastor with massive metal jaws as she jumped back. The beast glowed green in her vision, slinging him around and slamming him into the metal door frame edges repeatedly. Limbs severed, flying off the body in different directions, a leg landing with a thud inside the room. The demon tossed the lifeless body aside, turning its horrid gaze to Dee. A guttural growl reverberated inside the metal box as the creature lunged, slamming into the metal doorway. The frame bulged inward, jolting the safe house like a car wreck. Metal jaws snapped, blood dripping as it flailed and roared against the accidental steel trap.

They drew their sidearms, releasing a storm of small arms fire. Bullets bounced off the creature as it raged, clawing for entry.

Dee grimaced, snatching a nearby automatic rifle and squeezing off an entire clip into the demon until the tip glowed orange. Even so, it inched through the doorway, bending metal with each massive squirm. Her head throbbed in time with her elevated heartbeat as she went to one knee. The beast plunged into the makeshift safe house. She felt its pain.

Ko aimed over the sights of his giant sniper rifle as he yelled.

"Akujin!"

The creature glanced his way.

"Sayonara."

"Ko, wait!"

He pulled the trigger. Like a bomb, the percussive wave filled the room, rippling through her torso. The massive metal slug escaped the muzzle as hot gasses and flame spewed from the barrel. The recoil blew Ko back into the wall. Dee fell, ears ringing. Impact. The bullet grazed the armored headgear, scattering shield fragments before deflecting into the night.

The demon moved slower, shaking its head and offering a paltry growl as it stumbled toward Dee. Closer. Only steps away. She gaped in awe as she yanked the backup revolver from her ankle holster, targeting it from her fetal position. Her hand shook as she felt its anger and suffering, but also conflict. She thought for a moment it could sense her, too, until the gauntleted arm lifted to strike. Armor retracted from under the shoulder as thick, brown fur became visible. The mighty, reinforced arm reached its apex, ready to finish her.

A flash of metal as Ko swept in, swinging katana first into the exposed shoulder of the creature. Fur filled the air as the demon recoiled on hind legs. Ko sliced the belly three times. The demon repaid him with a massive swipe upward from the good arm. Ko crashed into the metal ceiling, his limp body following gravity down. His head bounced as his body impacted the floor. Ko laid still.

The demon's life force pooled on the floor as it stood on only three legs. Retreating toward the doorway, it exited the room and limp trotted away. Dee recovered, rushing to the side of her partner. She took his hand.

"Ko, no, what did you do?"

Ko bled from his chest through the tactical gear. His face swelling as arms and legs lay broken in the wrong positions. He turned to her, offering a painful smile as he gasped for air.

"Is okay. We're a very big deal."

"Better together. Remember?"

Ko exhaled his last, his head turning away from her. She grabbed his shoulders, shaking him.

"You hear me? Better together. Better together. Better..."

Her voice trailed off as she wept over his broken body. She placed her hands upon Ko's head and nodded, bowing for a moment of silence. Her facial muscles contorted around teary eyes. She screamed at the ceiling in agony and rage. Angry breaths fueled her before she rose from her departed friend.

As she stood, her eyes landed on the unopened bag of peanuts. She stared at them quietly with a wrinkled brow as her fingers formed a fist at her side. Her eye twitched.

"Anger may not control me, but it rules the night."

She opened her red clamshell device with blood-stained hands, tapping into StareFace as the technician had shown her.

Many graphs displayed on screen, and she clicked a spike in activity. She clicked again to a live satellite image. People entered the shed at the Mercer Mansion. Her face steeled as veins pulsed in her neck.

She dialed Butler. She spoke with a steady voice. Calm. Too calm.

"Director? Yes, it's me. No, the demon attacked. Ko is gone. Yes, moments ago."

Dee glimpsed the katana.

"No, sir. No backup needed."

She disconnected the phone and seized the sword. She turned the blade, studying it in the crimson light.

"Time to make my own mess."

CHAPTER 28

Kintaro Interlude Two

After years of training, Kintaro carried his own long sword on his back. He fought great battles with Master Miyamoto at his side, eventually becoming the powerful warrior known as Sakata Kintoki. Though they had vanquished menacing foes together throughout the land, he remained Kintaro in his own heart and mind. And Kintaro always kept his promises.

With his master aging, the time had come to take his mother to the mountaintop and recruit his own warriors, as he had promised those many years ago. Yet a recent threat prevented him from this task. A brutal ogre had risen from a lingering slumber, making the top of the mountain—his future home—unsafe.

The massive tyrant ripped ancient trees from the ground with gnarled bare hands, throwing them at houses as it screeched in otherworldly tongues.

When it yearned for meat, it ate animals from farms and slapped flocks of birds from the sky. Carcasses littered the forest. The poisoned excretions of the creature blighted the viridian landscape with yellowish brown death that fouled the air for days. As the abomination disrespected both nature and humanity, the mission to end it became essential.

Kintaro devised a plan to draw the creature out. With horsemeat being its favorite, volunteer riders on stallions would speed by the lair, luring it into the forest. There, in the relative protection of the enormous trees, he and his master would corner it to strike a final blow.

When the day arrived, a hoofed horde thundered by the cavern where the ogre lived. Unable to ignore such a bountiful feast, it emerged with great speed, pursuing them closely as they entered the tree line. As it got closer, the right moment approached. Miyamoto shrugged off his cloak, revealing himself as the rear rider. Leaping from his horse, he turned on the beast, attacking it with a flurry of katana slashes. He steadied himself with his second, smaller sword, burying it in hardened flesh as he traversed the creature. Though his attacks did not kill, they slowed the beast until it halted under the correct tree. The one Kintaro occupied. Dropping from a tall branch, he used gravity and skill as he plunged his own sword deep into the head of the creature, twisting it with all his might. The ogre fell with a thud that reverberated through the forest.

The plan had worked, but at significant cost. When the beast fell, the corpse crushed Miyamoto. Kintaro slashed at the carcass over and over in a mad fury. But try as he might, the helpless warrior could not flay enough thick flesh to reach his master in time. The onetime sword keeper had suffocated, giving his life so the people were finally safe. Kintaro and his aging mother did not forget his sacrifice as they sat on their porch with their animal friends, living in peace for the rest of their days.

CHAPTER 29

A shadow ran through the fields of the Mercer Mansion leading to the shed. The movement quickened, as if driven by an unseen hand. The specter stopped. It was Dee on a mission, camouflage paint covering her face. A tactical helmet and mandible guard enclosed her head. Full black assault gear encased her, dotted by the red clamshell tethered to her left shoulder.

Thirty feet from the shed, the grass rustled, sending her into hiding. Controlling her exhalations, she paused, hiding among the leaves and berries of nearby bushes. She peeked through the bramble from the shadows as two large men with rifles neared. They forced a third man to walk beside them, half-dressed with a black bag over his head. She squinted through the dark at the faces of the two large men—the redheaded farmer and the blond giant. The same men who had backed threats from Pastor Jimmy at the church. The redheaded one opened the shed door as the third man escaped, snatching the black bag off his head as he ran.

Tripping him, the blond giant smacked his head with the buttstock of a rifle. The bewildered face of the fidgety, long-haired man became clear as they dragged their buddy into the shed. The door closed behind them.

She paused, stunned by how quickly they had turned on their former ally. Jimmy said Knox wanted his people to cooperate if they stayed around—play to stay. What had this one done? Knox had not sent the creature. Was it already dead from Ko's earlier strikes?

Dee stepped out from the bushes, approaching the shed with light steps as she ogled the door. Gun raised, she grabbed the handle, throwing it open. No one. Dee scanned the compact interior with her rifle as before. The same table with a wench above and traps adorning the walls. A skeptical glance at the rug on the floor. Her eyes narrowed, focusing on a hinge system connecting the wooden legs to the ground. She tipped the table to the side, and the attached rug and support went with it. A staircase emerged. Dee pressed a button on the red clamshell, activating the underground radio.

"I'm going in. Keeping comms hot."

As she descended into the underground, the hidden entrance closed behind her.

Dee departed the last step into an austere tunnel lined with too many bright lights. She squinted as her eyes adjusted to the sterile space like a hospital waiting room. Square structural columns repeated along the walls. Cautious steps down the next hallway maintained her stealth, despite night gear contrasting against the stark white environment.

She reached a windowed meeting room. A quick peek. The redheaded church thug headed toward her, head down, as he reviewed a document. She ducked behind a support beam, drumming her rifle barrel guard. The conference door opened. She froze, gripping the long gun tighter as the man exited the room. He took a left down the hallway and around a corner. Dee exited her hiding place, entering the room before the door closed.

An underground war room greeted her. Antique dining chairs surrounded a large conference table on a gold fringed rug. Whiskey and bottled water topped an ornate wooden side table. Patriotic and military photography lined the wall. An illustration of a white dove holding a gun, smoking a cigar, and wearing a beret that read 'Let There Be Light.'

Dee circled the table. A homemade remote control with commands scribbled in German laid on it. She recognized three of the words. Attack. Charge. Hunt. She read the note beside it.

K, hope this helps your designs. -Denny

Photos, red string, and documents littered a massive corkboard on the wall. As Dee inspected it, her case became clearer. Photos of President Freeman and Isabel Ortiz next to Emperor Sakai. A string led to another photo of nuclear plant cooling towers.

Dee flipped through a document pinned to the board—energy contracts between the Freeman Foundation and the Government of Japan. As pages rustled between her fingers, she concluded that Freeman had been conducting business for his wife's organization on the country's dime.

Her eyes wandered to more photos with a red X crossed over them. Isabel's husband, Luis Ortiz. Pastor Jimmy and his wife, Angela Elliot. Ko Hashimoto. Dee touched Ko's image. Other photos of both her and Butler stared back, awaiting their own cross through. She leaned toward the red clamshell.

"Butler, you're on the kill board."

Images from other parts of the board rushed into her vision. Building schematics and aerial photos related to Brand Nuclear HQ in Reston.

"Why the hell are you using military reconnaissance on a business competitor, Knox?"

First Holiness of Rappahannock. Game warden Denny Lee. Sheriff Buddy Perry. State Police Headquarters in Virginia. The Lieutenant Governor. Mercer Energy HQ. Mercer Weapons Industries. Penny Mercer. The hooded man from the church.

All these people you own. Bought and paid for bootlickers. They won't save you today.

Dee exited with haste, following the path of the redheaded man. As she turned the corner, she encountered a massive old-fashioned wooden door, arched at the top and decked out in wrought iron. Gun at the ready, she pushed it open and entered.

As her eyes adjusted from the harsh lighting to semidarkness, the chamber came into view. Vintage lights gave off a warm glow, lining the stone walls of a circular room with caged holding cells at the edge. A massive chandelier hung from the middle of the domed ceiling, illuminating an elevated throne. Covered in gold leaf and animal furs, a metal gavel occupied the armrest. Bolted to the ground in front of the seat, a wooden pole with steel manacles.

Dee circled the room and found another hallway, but as she stepped into the path, a man's voice stopped her.

"Dead girl walking."

Turning back to the circular room, she scanned the dark cells at the edge of the room.

"That's right, over here."

Not aware of exactly where it originated, she dropped her night vision and wandered in the general direction of the voice.

"You walk through the valley of the shadow of death, you will have no comfort."

As she peered into the shaded cell, the fidgety church man, naked and shackled to the stone interior, bled from his forehead. Dee put a finger to her lips. Her helmet muffled her voice as she whispered.

"Quiet. I'll get to you later."

"No, you won't. We gotta be re-educated."

"Re-educated?"

"We are the light. You'll learn soon 'nough - the demon's gotta eat, too."

He grew bug-eyed, fixating on her as he broke into a ring-around-the-rosie song score.

"Demon's Gonna Get You. Demon's Gonna Get You. Demon's Gonna Get You."

She backed away. One step. Then another. His crazed cackles joined a struggle against his bonds, his frenzy turning songs to screams.

"Demon's Gonna Get You!"

Dee scanned the area as a skittish retreat led her to the other hallway. Passing through, she stopped short before entering the next room. She popped up her night vision. As her eyes adjusted to the brighter room, bloody sets of human-sized spiked crosses with iron chains stood unoccupied. Large metal rings and vintage electric lights covered the limestone walls. Someone had drawn seven large hash marks on the wall with chalk.

The gurgle of running water in a floor latrine near the wall permeated the space. It smelled grassy, like a natural stream. In the middle of the room, an elaborate metal altar with scrolled engravings sat integrated into the floor and ceiling. Sweeping steel buttressed it against the stone bricks and natural rock, integrating it into the room. Someone laid on the device, secured to the middle and dressed in a sheer white dress. Their arms and legs stretched as they shivered from the dampness.

As Dee approached, a helmet on the immobilized captive came into view. It enclosed their head except for a small hole. A red laser beam entered from the ceiling, where a single drop of water fell through the hole, landing with a plop. The woman cried out, and Dee recognized her.

"Penny?"

CHAPTER 30

Penny begged with a thready voice, "Make it stop. I promise to be a good girl."

Dee grabbed her knife, cutting through the bonds holding her distressed lover's arms and legs.

"Make the noises stop."

Stumbling over screws and latches, she removed the cover of the metal head restraint, tossing it to the side. The laser dot beamed directly on the forehead of the captive woman. A water drop fell from the ceiling, landing on the dot as Penny whimpered. She carried her limp, wet body to the corner and laid it gently against the wall.

"It's cold," Penny said, shivering against the stone.

Dee snapped and shook a portable hand warmer and gave it to her before removing a foil blanket from her pocket. She ripped the package open. As she unfolded it over Penny's cold, pale skin, the bruises from the earlier beating met her eyes. She lifted the dress hem slightly, revealing more purple marks. Dee scowled, coddling her by tucking the foil around her torso. Her hands moved over the thin cover and down her legs to her chilled feet.

"Where's Ko?" Penny asked.

Head down, the hardened hands of the agent paused on the wrapped feet of her one-night stand. Though she considered her more than that. Dee glanced up at her, shaking her head.

Lips quivering on her bruised face, Penny held back tears as she reached out to Dee. A mutual hug brought them cheek to cheek, eyes closed as both held back tears. Short, shallow gasps swelled longer as their embrace faded.

"Who did this to you?" Dee said.

"Buddy and his friends did this," Penny whispered, pointing to her face. "Dragged me to the water device. Strapped me down for re-education."

"Re-education?"

"A reset, inside, torture meant to break me down... I, I can't."

Penny dropped her head, covering her face. Dee lifted her chin and wiped a tear from her bruised cheek, caressing it as a tear came to her own eye.

"What else did they do?"

"Nothing else. This time," Penny paused, lip quivering for a tense moment. "None are innocent, Dee. Do you hear me? None of them."

Dee held her hand as she gritted her teeth.

"They will pay, I promise."

Penny offered a weak nod toward a different doorway.

"You're close. It's over there."

Dee tilted her head toward the massive steel bank vault door, already opened toward a pitch-black interior.

"What's in there?"

"Dad's demon."

Dee gently released Penny's hand as she stood. She flipped her night vision over her eyes as she stepped through the vault. Motion lights activated, forcing her to flip the goggles back. As her eyes adjusted, she trudged further into the shiny circular metal space. An armor-plated control room inhabited the middle with large, numbered cages along the edges.

Broad streaks of blood lined the floor leading to an enclosure labeled with the number one. As Dee scurried toward the central room, something yawned loudly in the distance. Her head started throbbing as she entered the control room. The panel inside sported multiple buttons. Her finger moved across one set labeled with numbers and another set of different colored buttons with multiple words. Fire. Spikes. Gun. Energy.

"It's a training room," she said, pressing button number one. Through the narrow window slits of the armored enclosure, she spied the massive cage door rising, ending its journey with a clang. The expected creature did not arrive.

Dee left the bunker, cautiously scanning the area as she approached the wide-open cage. Deep wheezing emanated from the blackness. She switched on the tactical light of her rifle, gritting her teeth as her headache grew. The beam landed on the face of the demon lying in a pool of blood. An immense metal helmet encircled its head. As the beast raised it, a single eye gazed at her before the head dropped with a mighty thud. A sorrowful moan echoed from the creature. Dee entered the cage, kneeling beside the behemoth.

As it twitched between soft growls, she laid her weapon and helmet to the side. With one eye on the demon, she ran her hand over the military armor plates covering it. She reached under one metal cover to touch the body of the creature for the first time. Thick, coarse fur pushed back against her hand as she stroked it. The demon grunted and sighed. Her fingers hit a hard bump. Eyebrows scrunched as she peered under the armor. An electrode sewn into shaved skin connected to wires embedded on the surface. Her hand followed them toward the head and a switch labeled with the word 'armed' beside a glowing red button.

Dee disconnected the headgear latches, the massive damage from the earlier rifle shot still visible. She yanked on the helmet. The demon pulled back. The headgear rolled away into the blood pool as she stood and backed away. She gasped. The broad head. Black nose. Rounded ears. Bright eyes. The creature looked at her, its enormous teeth offering the semblance of a grin instead of a snarl. The head dropped to the ground once again.

She returned, laying her hand on the side of its face as she caressed it. The giant bear closed its eyes at her touch. Dee mirrored it as the memories of the creature filled her. Seeing what it saw, she compared it to the hunting story Knox had shared.

***

Knox and his buddy walked through the wilderness, rifles at the ready. Knox kneeled to the ground, measuring a bear track.

"That's the one," he said.

As they came through to a clearing, a giant Kodiak bear and her two cubs searched the river. Fish flopped past, distracting the animals as the two men stopped short. Knox raised his gun. A second gun barrel rose beside it from the brush.

"We only need one," Knox whispered as he pulled, then pushed, the rifle bolt.

"Ready? 3. 2. 1."

As two shots resonated, the mother bear and one baby went down. Blood filled the surrounding water, mingling with bubbles downstream. The remaining cub sniffed at the dead sibling, pawing at the lifeless carcass. It turned toward mom, scampering to her and licking her face. It jumped on her unresponsive body until it tired and stood between its fallen family members, howling in agony. A net landed over it, cinching tight as they dragged it away.

***

Her head throbbing from the memory, Dee pondered the bear with a pitiful look. Torn from its family and experimented upon, she knew what this manipulated creature required of her. Its blood pooling on the floor, the agony of the animal transmitting to her in real time, she felt it all.

"I'll save you."

Dee slowly extracted the ancient katana her friend no longer needed. The one he had used to save her mere hours ago. She placed the tip of the sword by the bear's ribcage under the armor. After laying her other hand upon it, she bowed her head, offering a silent apology for the cruelty of the men who had perverted it. This fallen angel with fur. The work of genuine demons. She scowled as she plunged the sword deep into its chest cavity. The eyes and mouth of the animal grew wide before dimming and closing as the lifeless tongue hung to the side. Its lungs expelled their ultimate breath while Dee offered a last comfort in Japanese.

"Rest in Peace."

CHAPTER 31

As her mind quieted after slaying the demon, a creaky noise like a rusty wheel startled Dee. Still by the demon's side, she turned to Knox Mercer, rolling up in his wheelchair. A group of familiar faces gathered behind. Sheriff Buddy Perry—hat and all—held Penny in front of him as a human shield. Denny Lee escorted two German shepherds on each heel, eyes glowing red. The two church thugs—the redheaded farmer and the blond giant—drew their pistols.

"It seems we have a problem, Miss Dee," Knox said.

"Yes, Colonel, we do. You're a liar. And that chair isn't fooling anyone."

Knox looked around the room with a smirk on his face. Penny teared up as he locked the wheelchair in place with the handles, moving the footrests out of the way with his good leg. He pushed himself upward as his hidden second leg emerged from under him. Knox stood.

"Daddy? How long?" Penny said, trembling.

"Not now Penny!" He said, focusing on Dee. "First we must re-educate Miss Dee."

"No! No!" Penny pleaded, wriggling against the sheriff's grip.

Buddy smacked her in the ear.

"Hush now, you deceitful slut!"

Penny seethed from his slap.

"You brought her here with your sinful ways," Knox said, turning to his daughter for the first time. "No matter how often my friends and I disciplined you, you always backslid into your vile and scurrilous actions."

"Disciplined?" Penny ridiculed through tears, her southern accent growing thicker as she raged against her captor. "Mom died and you let these psycho shits violate and abuse me." Dee made a fist as Penny exposed her pain. "Dressed me up as something I'm not since high school! I'm not your fucking toy doll to do with whatever you want!"

Knox scoffed.

"We tried to make you something special. Trained you properly. You could have had anyone. Done anything," Knox said, pointing to Dee.` "Her death? And that of the creature? This house is awash in your sins, you worthless brat. And now payment has come due."

Penny locked eyes with Dee, mouthing, 'I'm sorry' before hanging her head. Over her sniffling, Knox continued preaching.

"You imagine we are simple, Miss Dee, but nothing is ever what it seems... is it, former agent? You're Freeman's dirty little secret, cast overboard like bad bait. No wonder you don't understand nuclear energy would ruin us around here. Without coal, well, I don't exist. We'd be half as large and twice as dumb. This entire region depends on it for our livelihood. But those traitors in DC don't get that. The President had to try the Hail Mary in Tokyo on his way out. Well, things could have been different. The demon should have been there."

Dee fixated on Knox as rage filled her face. Memories of that night in Tokyo flooded into her mind as she completed the blanks on her own.

***

Dee opened a limo door.

The President turned to face her.

"Mr. President, time to go home."

Dee reached out her hand.

The President took it, exiting the limo.

"Wait! No!" Ko yelled.

A bullet hit her.

Blood sprayed the President.

Dee went down.

An eagle flock swarmed.

The sniper fast roped down the building.

Entering a vehicle, they removed the mask.

Knox Mercer.

***

The one who had caused her recent pain stood feet away, ready for her justice. Dee had practiced killing on those deemed worthy by her government. On the battlefield. In the streets abroad, where uprisings and insurrections abounded. Yet there could be no more honorable kill than old man Mercer after his treatment of Penny and the bullet to her own shoulder. Her mind sizzled with revenge as her heart pumped with payback. Yet he was also the man she could not kill. Her deal with Butler constrained her actions. She would take Knox alive. The others warranted no such protection.

"We are a light in a world of shadows, Miss Dee," Knox said. "Tokyo failed, but Ortiz was a solid second prize. Fresh meat for the demon."

Knox turned to his two church thugs.

"Time to re-educate her, boys. Let there be light."

"No! Let there be dark," she said, smacking the EMP button on the back of the lifeless armored bear and rolling behind it. The lights went out as she flipped her night vision goggles down.

The church thugs shot blindly at her previous spot.

Denny ordered in German, "Attack!"

Canine eyes glowed green in her vision. Dee, crouching behind the carcass, drew her 1911 side arm and canceled the canine attack with two precision shots each. She holstered the pistol, snatching the sword from the demon's corpse as she rushed the reloading thugs. She slid on her knees between them, slicing one of their shin bones with a katana swing while severing the second thug's leg at the knee with the backswing. Both thugs fell, screaming in pain, as she spun around to a stop.

Dee kipped to her feet, stabbing one in the chest with the blade as she screamed a murderous yell. Snatching the 1911 from her holster, she aimed. The other thug took a bullet to the head.

Blinded by the dark, Denny snatched his Ka-Bar knife from a leg sheath. She jumped at his upper body, locking the knife wielding limb in an arm bar. Arching her back, she cracked his limb, dislocating his elbow. Denny screamed, dropping the knife. She judo rolled toward it, grabbed it, and threw it at the sheriff. He kneeled as he screamed from the impact, his impaled leg spurting blood into the dark as Penny escaped from his grasp until Knox snatched her. Dee stood, shooting Denny at close range. Two in the chest. One in the head. His limp body fell to the ground.

The pistol slide locked back. She threw the empty 1911 at Buddy's head, knocking off his hat. He grabbed his head as he seethed, the head wound competing for supremacy with the knife in his leg. He shuddered. Someone pulled close. Dee whispered from the dark.

"The place where the noises are."

A single katana swing and the sheriff's head bounced and rolled away.

Knox and Penny stood close together in her night vision. Dee threw out a handful of firefly chem-lights. As their green light emanated from every direction, Knox held Penny captive at knifepoint. Penny dug her fingernails into the arm around her neck, her taut brow begging silently for help. Dee pointed the sword at Knox. He pushed his own Ka-Bar blade harder into her neck, liberating a tiny blood trickle.

"I'll do it. You know I will!" Knox said.

Dee stared Knox down, holding the katana as intense gulps of underground air fueled her fury. She eyeballed him while pressing a button on her red clamshell device.

"Butler, my room's a mess."

CHAPTER 32

After Dee called for backup on the red clamshell, a laser dot appeared immediately on Penny and Knox. Dee peeked over her shoulder. Emerging from the shadows, Director Butler shouldered a rifle as he peered through its holographic sights.

"Copy on that cleanup, Wildcat, five by five."

Her face contorted, still pointing the sword toward Knox with her quivering arm.

"That was quick," Dee said.

"Hey, award me janitor of the year. You can drop that salad shooter, I got him."

Dee placed the sword on the ground.

"He'll kill me, Dee. He will kill all of us!" Penny said.

Dee peered at Knox.

"Your dad may have lost. But regardless of your history, he doesn't want you dead. Isn't that right, Colonel?"

"Not my dad. Him!" Penny said, nodding to Butler.

Dee stood speechless as the red dot of Butler's weapon moved to Penny's shoulder. Penny dug fingernails into her father's arm. Dee pivoted to Butler, unarmed, eyes widening, heart pumping as Butler pulled the trigger.

Penny cried out as her shoulder absorbed the slug. Knox took two more to the torso. Dee spun back as Penny fell to the ground, bleeding out on her white dress. Penny laid still as Knox stumbled back, kneeling from the impact as he ripped his shirt, revealing a bulletproof vest. Director Butler turned the rifle on Dee.

"Damn it, Knox. Look at this mess."

"Goddamn it, Sean. What are you doing here?"

Dee's jaw dropped.

"You know each other?"

"Yeah, I know this son-of-a-bitch," Knox said. "If he had deployed the prototype in Tokyo, like I said, we would be golden right now."

"The prototype wasn't ready, and we couldn't risk it out in the open," Butler said.

"You benched the beast for a flock of birds."

"You seemed to use them well enough."

"Admit it," Knox said, placing the knife back into his leg sheath. "The big job scared you."

"Who used advanced weapons tech for their business ventures and local politics? You risked everything, Colonel."

"We can't be in the shadows forever. Now end her and let's get back on track."

With hands raised, Dee chastised her old boss through shallow breaths.

"My God. What have you done, Sean?"

"Yeah, Sean," Knox said, grimacing as he stood. "Might want to break it down Barney-style, Marine!"

"Oh, she's bright enough to catch on, aren't you, agent?"

Dee took a moment as she considered this newfound association. She eyeballed the Ka-Bar knives on both of their legs.

"Two hunting buddies," Dee said. "You met while serving in the Marines. Colonel's older... probably your commanding officer. Kindred spirits who both went hard on the world. You didn't like how it was changing."

"Told you she would catch on fast," Butler said.

Dee paced as she spoke, glancing occasionally at Penny.

"You needed to make the world safe—like you imagined it used to be. But the politicians couldn't be bothered with bold moves. At least not bold enough for you. And when the Mercer family fortune flowed to Knox, it funded a perfect partnership to experiment, torture or kill as you saw fit."

As she filled in the blanks further, the Alaskan hunting ground where Knox encountered the bear became clearer in her mind. She imagined how it probably went.

***

A giant Kodiak and her two cubs fished in the river. The two hunting companions paused. Knox raised his gun as he whispered.

"We only need one."

Knox pulled and pushed the rifle bolt.

A second barrel rose.

"I got the little one," Butler said.

"Ready? 3. 2. 1."

Two shots rang out.

***

"StareFace. The Demon. Two different tools, part of a complex arsenal for one simple end. Control. Starting with government energy contracts. Nuclear be damned. How did I do, Marines?"

"Now that's a beautiful brain," Knox said, shaking his head and leering. "Just like the rest of her. It was smart to keep her on the sidelines."

"Yeah, she got most of it," Butler said. "Missed the part where she and I get rich selling StareFace intel to the highest bidder."

"That's me," Knox said.

"It used to be," Butler said as his rifle laser landed on Knox's forehead.

"What's this shit, Marine?!"

Dee creeped toward the sword on the floor.

"The spoils of war. I found another buyer, and you're a liability," Butler said, gripping the rifle tighter. "Capture Ortiz. Capture! Not kill her in her own goddamned house. And now what? You want to stuff me, too? I was high over Tokyo when that shit blew, and you knew it."

"Well, you got me," Knox chided. "So, what are you gonna do? My money. My politicians."

"Ha, the last words of a grand old man. That's the agency's money now. Which makes it my money. And politicians always follow the—"

"Powerful men always think they're in control, don't they, Sean?" Dee said.

Butler glanced over to her before refocusing on Knox.

"That's right, men like Knox. Freeman. The rich. The privileged. They couldn't even wipe without people like me. Like us."

"And upstart idiots like Isabel Ortiz never stood a chance, am I right?" Dee said.

"Damn straight. Bunch of losers."

"Although, you know, they may not agree," Dee said, leaning her head close to the red clamshell device on her left shoulder.

"Isn't that right, Mr. President?"

Over the speaker, President Freeman said, "Always happy to hear about my failures, Agent Johnson. How about you, Señora Ortiz?"

"Right on, Mr. President."

Director Butler's face turned empty.

Dee grinned at Butler, tapping the red clamshell.

"The radio works underground, or so I've been told, ex-Director."

Butler bristled at her veiled insult as Freeman spoke.

"Sorry I can't join that welcome wagon headed your way, agent. But we will always have Tokyo."

"Always have Tokyo," Butler said, echoing the President. "Always have Tokyo. It's a goddamned code."

"It's also math," Dee said. "A person attacked by a shark, that's rare. But two attacks by the same shark? Like hot peanuts on Pluto."

CHAPTER 33

Butler refocused his rifle muzzle on Knox. Dee eyeballed her old boss, inching toward the sword she had dropped earlier. The red laser dot found the old Colonel's wrinkled temple. His eyes expanded as Butler locked aim. Dee dropped to a knee, grabbing the katana as a shot rang out. Knox fell.

Butler glanced at Dee as she hurled the sword at him. He recoiled as the katana barely sliced his arm before bouncing off the metal wall. He seethed, turning to the exit as he bled. Dee judo rolled to an enemy pistol and snatched it. One missed shot hit the wall by his head as he escaped through the giant bunker door. The slide on the gun had locked back. She threw it down before moving to Penny.

Dee placed her hand on Penny's wrist, checking her pulse briefly before moving on to her shoulder. It still bled from Butler's earlier rifle shot. She placed a nerve block patch on the arm before snatching XStat sponge syringes from her field pouch. As Dee injected the wound, the bleeding slowed, then stopped. Penny rolled her head toward her, eyes filled with relief as Dee stroked her fiery red hair.

"I promise." Dee inhaled sharply. "You'll be okay, I promise."

An announcement came over her radio, "Five minutes out."

Dee stood, grabbing her rifle. She checked the ammo count before exiting the room after Butler.

In the re-education room, the vintage lights lining the stone walls had burned out from the EMP blast. With her night vision enabled, Dee saw the bloody set of spiked crosses with chains. And once again, the torture device they had used on Penny. One more hash mark lined the wall. She moved her hand on the chalk marks as her eyes narrowed under the goggles. He had been tracking his kills. The sound of running water in the nearby floor latrine masked her hearing, hypnotizing her for a moment. She thought of Ko and Penny, but recalling her dad broke her oddly calm trance. With new focus, she raised her rifle.

Stepping through the darkened hallway, she sighted down the gun, gritting her teeth. She penetrated the rotunda where the man had sung to her earlier. His disturbing words had motivated her. *Demon's gonna get you.* She labeled him a false prophet.

Boom! A flash-bang grenade blinded her. She recoiled from the pain in her eyes, and a rifle buttstock knocked her fuzzier. After her body crashed to the ground, Butler kicked her rifle away and clutched her collar, dragging her across the floor. Dee felt the ground slide underneath her boots. He propped her up on her knees. Cold steel met her wrists.

"Two minutes out."

Butler swiped her red clamshell device, slamming it on the ground. He stomped it with his boot heel twice before shooting it with his 1911.

"Monitor that, you fucks!"

As Dee returned to consciousness, she startled against the chains and old manacles at the foot of the central throne. Butler strutted by, heading toward the elaborate chair. Blurry in her vision, he hopped onto it and pressed buttons. On the massive chandelier hanging from the domed ceiling, the lights brightened as he turned a knob. He extracted a cigar and lighter from a pouch attached to the armrest. Smoke rose from the familiar perch toward the stone dome as he took the metal gavel and banged it on the armrest.

"Court is now in session."

The church man sang from his cage once again.

"Demon's Gonna Get You. Demon's Gonna Get—"

"The demon's dead, you idiot!" Dee said.

"No, he's not. The demon's on the throne!"

She glanced at Butler.

Butler shrugged.

"Don't worry, when your friends get here, death will come for us all. Fortunately for the world, my legacy transcends death."

Butler puffed his cigar, illuminating his fevered eyes.

"Disinformation, agent. That's the key. Keep it focused. Narrowing the average person's field of view can be of extreme usefulness. Ninety percent of the information you let through might be the absolute, irrefutable truth. But that last ten percent you mix in? Not lies, but a poisoned truth that destroys reason and reality. Wow! I mean, you name it. Election doubts. Digital currency stability. An ancient demon. The bozos believe all that bull."

Butler raised his palms to the ceiling. Cigar still in hand, he smiled, closing his eyes as he turned his head upward.

"It's like that old TV show. I want to believe."

"Patronizing fuck," Dee said. As her vision cleared, movement in the shadows found her eyes, barely visible opposite her in the rotunda.

Butler took another puff and eyeballed her. His mocking tone turned more serious.

"The lies we believe tell us much about ourselves, agent. The ones we mutually commit to tell us about our society. This prototype worked out the quirks, but we needed a cover story for field testing. So, we queued up some old tale about a native forest demon. Ha! Anyone researching it would have found it online. That's the beauty, the lie feeds on itself."

The shadowy thing drew closer as Butler continued.

"Plus, we leveraged the increasing animal attacks happening in national forests. They occur with greater frequency than most know. Anyone curious enough could do the research and find irrefutable proof—at least irrefutable to them—that supported their theories. Those who didn't want to use those explanations to be part of my team, well, we just sprinkled in threats of violence. A dash of bribes. Mixed messages across channels. The local church. The news props. Government agency alliances. You know, nation building 101? You've done it, too. When you were Delta Force. If we can do it to Uganda, Taiwan, or the Kashmir, we can do it to this state."

He puffed on the cigar as Dee eyeballed the specter, moving ever closer.

"But the data is the real prize. Our research will fuel animal weapon science for decades. Bombs on dolphins? Cold War nonsense. Drones? Target practice for wannabes in some desert shit hole."

He waved his hand as if painting his envisioned world.

"Imagine it, militarized herds for profit. Wild horses tamed and remote-controlled in Mexico. Mechanized elephants stampeding the enemy in Africa. An army of macaques in India? Hell, those little shits already attack people for potato chips. There are more kangaroos in Australia than the population of Alabama. God made all animals for us to rule. But with them at our side? We rule everything. With them at our side, we are gods."

Butler placed the cigar on an armrest and grabbed an electronic device from another pouch. As he manipulated the remote control, her head throbbed. How was the pain getting worse? Her eyesight had cleared quickly after his ambush. She did not have a concussion.

Then it emerged, revealing furry claws and a tawny coat. Bright eyes and a lengthy tail all shrouded in military-grade armor. Butler moved a joystick on the controller, and it charged. Her head pounded. Agile and fast, it started its leap. As she accepted her death, the mechanized cougar stopped. It shivered, shaking its head. She felt the pain of the implants in the creature. The modern beast sensed her. Her ability to feel it reflected to the animal. It growled and hissed as it paced, but it did not direct its anger at her.

"You like her?" Butler said, fidgeting with the remote. "We named it Hera because, well, you'll find out when I fix this shoddy piece of junk."

"That's not her name," Dee said, cocking her head.

Butler glanced up from the device. "No?"

"No, she won't tell me her actual name. But she said she has plans for you."

Butler raised an eyebrow.

"Told me you stole her from her family," Dee said. "Put these gadgets on her. Injected her with chemicals, drugs, and viruses. Made her something sick and twisted. Your friend made her kill someone on a trail. I can only assume it was Angela Elliott? Pastor Jimmy's wife."

Butler scoffed.

"Well, that's a hell of a story, agent. What else did she tell you?"

"That she hates you. For thinking you own her. And that given the choice, she would bite your throat clean out."

The giant cat locked eyes with Butler, dropping its head and arching its back. Butler fiddled with the remote, but the cat remained focused on him as it stalked nearer. He drew his 1911 pistol. The cougar charged. He pulled the trigger over and over in a rapid burst, emptying the forty-five-caliber gun into the feline attacker, leaping through the air. Armor deflected metal as the massive cat pounced, grabbing his neck. Butler flailed as the cat snarled, panting through nostrils filling with blood. He grabbed the Ka-bar knife from his leg sheath, flailing against the creature with meager stabs as his neck flesh ripped. The cougar flung his trachea across the room. Butler went limp, his knife bouncing on the floor as red liquid streamed over the golden throne. Face and body covered in gore, the muscular feline dismounted and snarled a painful cry.

Dee teared up, relieved it was over, but emotionally spent from the pain transferred to her. She dislocated her thumb and removed the chains binding her. Steadying herself as she stood, she spoke through gritted teeth toward the corpse of her old boss.

"Powerful men always think they're in control."

In the distance, Penny stood inside the rotunda. Holding her arm, she limped slightly under her blood-stained dress. Dee did not know how long she had been there or what she had seen, but it did not matter as she closed the distance between them. They embraced, eyes shutting as they hugged each other tight. The cougar pawed gently at Dee's leg. She kneeled to stroke it.

"I know people who can fix you," she said, hugging the weary, bloody animal as it purred.

CHAPTER 34

Dee startled awake in her seat. She instinctively grabbed for the long, thin case leaning against the wall of the train car. Glancing around, everyone scrolled devices, paying her no attention. Still, she felt both invisible and conspicuous at the same time. A walking contradiction, though her formal black pantsuit blended well with the Japanese business travelers. She turned toward the scenery outside her window, whizzing by on the trip from Narita to Bunkyo City. Her somber face stared back at her in the reflection. Drifting in and out after the long flight, her eyes closed. She dreamed of her last time in Tokyo, replaying it in her mind. The time Ko came to her in the hospital. The bullet around her neck. His masterful attack against the giant bear. Yet he called *her* Kintaro.

Ding!

Dee roused, looking out the window again. The buzz of the city greeted her. A voice spoke in

Japanese over the speaker, "Next stop, Otsuka-ekimae Station."

She gathered a small backpack and slung the thin case over her shoulder before exiting the train.

Inside the station, people filled the space. Two brushed against her as they rushed into their day. Everyone wore black suits or dresses, crowding each other while remaining civil. Moving with the flowing river of humanity, Dee neared a luggage locker. She swiped her phone over the payment slot and opened the gray box. Placing her backpack on the table, she removed a Kintaro Adventures children's book from her backpack. She opened the front cover.

Inside was a note she had written to Ko.

Dear Ko,

Safe travels, my nutty friend.

Jikai,

Dee 'Kintaro' Johnson

Dee tucked a condolence money envelope inside the book and closed it. She placed the backpack in the locker and locked it.

***

With hundreds of others, Dee stood across the street from the Gokokuji temple entrance. The dark red wooden edifice topped with gray slate tiles contrasted against the glass and metal buildings nearby. As the signal changed, the crush of humanity drove her past Shinobazu-dori Avenue. She marched through the y-shaped intersection with the book in hand and the thin case on her back until the entrance grew large in her vision. She remained stoic outside, absorbing the sight as mourners streamed through the Torii gate dressed in black. Komainu stone dogs faced each other as the street traffic resumed behind her.

Entering the temple grounds, throngs of funeral-goers washed their hands using the hishaku ladle before stepping deeper into the courtyard. A sinewy metal robot with no eyes played the Koto near the entrance. Dee integrated into the crowd, standing many rows deep. A modestly dressed person approached, working his way through the crowd. He offered a brief bow.

"I am the assistant, please come, Johnson-san."

She followed him across the courtyard. Cherry blossoms adorned their path, new petals dropping. His pace quickened.

They entered the wake room, where a much smaller group sat in rows. At the entryway, a man sat behind a table where piles of condolence money envelopes laid. Dee opened the book and handed her envelope to him. He offered a slight bow from his seated position as he took it before the assistant walked her toward the front of the room.

As she followed, a white coffin with blue embroidery surrounded by ornate flower arrangements became clearer. Standing in front of it, a painted portrait of Ko looked back at the audience. A spirit tablet inscribed with a name and the family crest in Kanji. The assistant stopped as Dee followed.

He turned, motioning for her to sit in the front row. Dee looked at the only chair available next to an elderly Japanese man. His face worn as old burlap. He looked up at her, his eyes bright with tears. It was the father, Saburo.

"Please, honor us," he said simply.

Dee sat in the honored spot beside the father. The crowd settled as the wake began. Stepping forward, the Shinto Priest adorned in white garments and a tall thin black hat chanted selections of the Sutra as the mourners looked on. Upon completing them, Saburo stood and waited.

He looked down at Dee and offered his arm. Remembering the party where she had rejected the same gesture from Ko, she took the father's arm. Together they stepped to the brass incense urn in front of the coffin. The elder Hashimoto sprinkled powdered incense three times in a row. He signaled to Dee. She mirrored the ceremony.

As they moved to the side of the coffin, the body of her old partner came into view. A white kimono wrapped him right over left under folded hands holding white prayer beads. Saburo placed flowers, filling the empty spaces around the face of his son. Dee placed the book on his chest, tapping it as if to secure it in place for all time.

Saburo turned to Dee, holding both hands out. Dee removed the thin case from behind her back. She then handed the sword and sheath to the father with a slight bow. He placed it on the body, the handle resting near the hands of his son. As they returned to their seats, all stood to join them. Assistants holding rocks hammered the coffin shut. The priest led the entourage outside as the helpers rolled the coffin out of the room. They looked on as the rear door of the shiny black hearse opened, accepting the coffin before slamming shut.

Koto music wafted through the air as the bulbul birds chirped from the Sakura trees. The growing throng at the temple crowded to the side as the funeral procession turned the corner. The priest in white walked toward the masses with deliberate steps, head down and holding the Shaku wooden mace. Younger priests dressed in gray followed behind. The chrome on the tall black hearse sparkled in the sun as courtyard gravel groaned under the lumbering vehicle tires. Cherry blossom petals filled the early spring air as breezes flowed through the temple grounds. Trudging alongside the hearse, the shiny shoes of mourners became speckled with dust.

As they passed, the robot playing the Koto stopped and bowed toward the poignant spectacle. The elder Hashimoto and Dee walked alongside the hearse as it proceeded past the multitude.

"Ko called you Kintaro," Saburo said stoically in Japanese. "His mother told him that story often. Did he tell you what it was about? What the ending meant?"

Dee recalled the book she had laid with Ko. It was in Kanji. She could not read it. But she remembered the road to Castleton—after the gas attendant—and how Ko had shared the story with her.

"The master and Kintaro slayed the ogre," she said.

"True, that happened. But what is the story about?"

Dee paused for a moment. His quizzical approach had confused her. Though tired, she considered this could be his way of grieving and remembrance.

"The master died, but the student survived," she said.

"Yet the story is not about victory."

"What then, Hashimoto-san?"

"Sacrifice."

Dee nodded, "Your son's sacrifice for me."

"Cherish the gift of my son. Do not waste it."

He placed his hand on her shoulder as he spoke.

"Do not worry. Ko is strong, like Onikuma. Strength of ten men."

Did he speak about his deceased son in the present tense by accident?

"Onikuma?" Dee asked.

Ko's father gave the smallest smile ever. He removed his hand and swept it around as both their eyes followed.

"The Kami. The spirit world. There, he is a giant bear. He sleeps now. Rests in caves behind waterfalls. But not forever."

She closed her eyes, turning to the blue sky and allowing the sun to drench her face. Pausing in the moment, she absorbed the world around her before returning attention to him.

"You believe he will return? One day?"

"No. I believe he never left."

CHAPTER 35

The door to her room at the hospital radiology suite closed after the nurse left. Dee heard the sliding doors of the hospital exits every time someone passed. Outside the window, squeaky wheelchairs rolled by as orderlies in patterned scrubs pushed patients to vehicles filled with their expectant families. Dee pulled the candy bar from the pocket of her athletic wear, hoping to quench the burned coffee taste from her tongue. She had grabbed it from the vending machine before the scan, the results of which she dreaded as she took a bite. Chocolate crumbled onto the paper covering the medical table.

After deciding to seek an official medical diagnosis for her headaches and panic attacks, she had also vowed to keep it quiet. Whatever the outcome of her tests, she alone would reveal results—in her own time and to whom she chose.

The door opened. As her physician approached, gray hair and kind, azure eyes complemented his sympathetic, but crinkled, visage.

"Jada White?" He said, addressing Dee by the alias she had provided. "I'm Dr. Henry."

He extended his palm. It reminded her of a chilled fish reeking of antiseptic as she shook it. He enabled a wall screen and steered a stool toward it. Medical test images filled the monitors.

"There is no easy way to say it, so I'll be straight with you. You have brain cancer," the doctor said, pointing to a scan. "Specifically, a slow-growing tumor called an astrocytoma brought on by Li-Fraumeni syndrome or LFS."

Dee sat stunned at the diagnosis. She had never heard of LFS and certainly never thought cancer would be the culprit in her panic attacks.

"I've passed all my physicals. I feel mostly healthy, just headaches and a sore shoulder. How did this happen now?"

"LFS is an inherited predisposition to a wide range of cancers. There is a gene called TP53 that suppresses tumor formation, but in people with LFS it is mutated, inhibiting its function."

"Are you sure about the diagnosis?"

"The scans seem definitive, but gene sequencing will confirm. Individuals with LFS have a fifty percent chance of developing cancer by age forty, and a ninety percent chance by age sixty. You are lucky to have made it this far without symptoms. It can manifest at a young age. However, there's a more fascinating aspect to your diagnosis. Your tumor's morphology is unique."

"Morphology?" Dee said, raising an eyebrow.

"The way it looks. Your patient history says you're a consultant?"

"That's right."

"I don't want to put you in a tough position," Dr. Henry said, smiling. "But have you ever served in the military? Particularly special ops?"

Dee sat silent, trapped in her thoughts. She could not say yes, but she needed to know the relevance of his question.

"I can't tell you that, but what if I did?"

"Well, if you did, then you certainly received military-grade anti-fungal injections. These were meant for desert warfare since that is where most fungi like *Candida auris* and *Aspergillus* started taking hold in the 2020s. There are activist lawsuits around the country claiming those treatments amplified cancer incidence in veterans. When we ran your scans through the medical imaging AI for confirmation of diagnosis, we found a study out of China. It highlights interactions with mutated TP53 proteins and similar anti-fungals, but their theories encompassed more than the cancer."

"What else were they studying?"

"Well, what you described when you first arrived. Headaches. Hallucinations. Out of body experiences, like remote viewing the world through the eyes of other creatures. There is only one study, and it was not peer reviewed, so I don't know what to believe. I have colleagues in China, some were authors on the paper. It makes me uncomfortable to even cite it."

"Why, what did they say?"

"The unique experience that anti-fungals and TP53 provide only happens in women. The Chinese group started the study on young girls. They identified TP53 mutations and injected them with surplus military-grade anti-fungals not sanctioned for children. Then they followed that cohort through to the age of thirty, tracking this animal sensory perception bridge all while denying them treatment along the way. They let it go too long. Every one of them likely died horribly since the study data ends prematurely."

"Jesus. Kids? Why? Why would they do that and publish it? I feel sick."

"I know how you feel. Good science can go bad fast. Certain economies have grown so large they are immune to scrutiny by the scientific community. China. America. India. It is easy to take science too far with infinite dollars and minimal oversight."

Taking it too far? Dee imagined her hands wrapped around the neck of two or three cruel scientists. The thought of liberating mistreated girls, many of them like her, gave her joy. Her heart burned with vengeance as her mind sizzled. She liked the feeling and held it close for later.

"That's truly awful, but is there is a cure in my case?"

"Removal of the malignant tissue and radiation is the most aggressive course of treatment. However, since this type grows slowly, we can also watch and wait if you prefer. That would be my recommendation. Either way, it will catch up with you, eventually."

"How long do I have, doc?" Dee asked, wringing her hands.

"Once LFS patients develop symptoms from the cancer, it isn't long before it pops up elsewhere. I would say five years at most. When your symptoms get worse, you won't be able to function without help. You need to prepare for that and the treatments that follow."

Once Dee heard the timeframe, her internal clock started ticking as a stopwatch instead of a time bomb. Like a fast-burning candle, she knew one day her light would extinguish for good. But she still had time to live a life. She felt free. Liberated from duty for the first time in a long while.

"We can watch and wait," Dee said.

"Good, I will adjust your medi-lot with a different pain medicine. And I would avoid your, uh, consulting work for a while. I'll have the nurse schedule your quarterly follow up."

After he washed his hands, he left the room. Dee hopped off the patient table. No one saw her exiting the room as she scurried through the external sliding doors. She marched briskly through the parking lot to her SUV.

"Drive randomly," she said before the vehicle pulled away.

She closed her eyes, breathing in and out slowly as her psy-bot had instructed. Again she breathed. And again.

"I am worthy of happiness."

She opened her eyes.

Jo, are you there?

Yes, Dee, I'm here. How can I help?

I just found out I have cancer.

I'm sorry to hear that, Dee.

I guess I'm lucky, or so the doctor said. I could have gotten it much earlier in life.

Are you thankful for the time you've been given?

You know what? I am. A lot of it has been ripe garbage, but there have been a lot of exceptional moments, too. I'll have to make a few more before I go.

Would you like to share your prognosis with me, Dee?

The doctor said five years. Could be more, but probably less. I think he was trying to stay positive, Jo. For my sake.

Five years. Fifteen percent more of life to live!

Living it fiercely, Jo. Guess what I won't need in five years?

I don't know. What?

You, ha!

Ha, now that is a good joke, Dee.

CHAPTER 36

The sun rose over Dee jogging along the familiar sidewalk of Minnesota Avenue just outside of DC. Cars passed her one after the other, but the morning commute did not concern her today. She had other plans. Wind breezed by as she sprinted to the last intersection before home. Her new, slick running garb made her feel faster, though her times got slower with each passing year. Full gasps filled her lungs as headphones blasted her favorite soundtrack. She swigged a drink from her water bottle.

From the corner of her eye, two suited men watched her from across the street. One touched their ear. She glanced over her shoulder. Another man. Her heart rate, already high, spiked a bit more. Their positioning and communication approach screamed Secret Service. Uncertainty rose like the sun. Her eyes narrowed as she capped her water bottle and pulled her earbuds out. Engine sounds and screeching tires startled her as a limousine and two large SUVs pulled into the intersection. The door of the limo opened, and another agent stepped out. Behind him, President Freeman motioned for her to enter the vehicle.

As Dee sat, the agent slammed the door behind her. The motorcade charged away.

"Mr. President?" Dee said, pausing briefly. "Water?"

She tilted the half-empty bottle toward him.

"I'm good. What are you listening to?"

"You wouldn't believe me if I told you."

The President smirked.

"And your treatments at the Foundation? Are they helping the headaches?"

"Haven't started yet, but the pains seem to have gone away. I'll call to schedule a checkup with Reggie and Sam."

He snatched a remote and activated a monitor that dropped from the ceiling. Dee turned her attention to the screen as Isabel Ortiz waved to a crowd from a stage filled with balloons and supporters. She held a photo of Luis close to her. The lower third of the screen read 'Isabel Ortiz wins in Landslide.'

"You did that," Freeman said.

"Glad you got her out in time."

"We were lucky. The threat went deeper than we knew. More people died than we wanted. But it had to stay covert. I didn't know who to trust. Glad we had an operative in Butler's organization to leverage his feud with Mercer."

"Mika Hinode—the teenage girl—if that's even her real name and age?"

"It's not. Don't let youthful appearances fool you. She accomplished two major goals—shepherding those Level-4 devices to you and securing video of Knox using the creature haphazardly. Getting you the devices was easy with anti-surveillance prototypes courtesy of the Freeman Foundation."

"Neat trick, Mr. President."

"Whereas Knox exploiting the demon without Butler's okay inflamed his rage and primed him for our own little disinformation campaign. Luring him in and securing a monitored confession was icing."

"Destroying reason and reality was Butler's specialty. That's an outcome you can't even achieve with bombs. Rooting him out before leaving office was a big win, Mr. President. Even though he was a mole, I'm glad he got to us before Knox. It bought us time. What about the others he hinted at?"

"Enablers of his organization, foreign or domestic, will see justice. Vice President Webb will make sure of it once he's inaugurated. Unfortunately, Butler's meddling will force us to scrub a generation of animal weaponization, intelligence, and monitoring systems. We simply can't trust those platforms anymore. You—you both—went beyond the call to keep comms hot and play bait. I just wanted to say thank you, in person."

Dee swigged her water.

"So, it is official then, Mr. President?"

"All negative marks have been redacted from your record. So, my next question is why aren't you taking the position with us? You wanted to settle down a bit, or so I thought."

"Yes, I suppose that means something different for me now. I've grown tired of being controlled by... I don't know... by flawed masters. No offense to you, sir."

"None taken."

"I'm not innocent," Dee said, wringing her well-worn hands. "But I hoped for the best, only to find the worst. I guess my trust in people has turned thin. And now it's time for a recharge. For a change."

"My dad used to say, 'Be the change that you wish to see in the world.' "

"That's Gandhi, isn't it?" Dee said, raising an eyebrow.

"Yes, but the benefits of that change depend on one's perspective. A feast for one is a famine for another. Leaving may work for you, but I'm losing a fantastic agent."

Dee accepted his praise graciously, but it did not alter her decision. He used flattery like any superb politician—to get his way. As much as she liked him personally and professionally, she could never fully trust him. A flawed master. That phrase perfectly described her feelings toward him. Flawed like all leaders that came before and all that would come after.

"Speaking of change," Freeman said, tapping a button on his console. "It's a bittersweet election week for me. My legacy is secure as Butler's terrorist network collapses. I can start moving past the presidency while taking my farewell tour. Pump up my wife's Foundation. Fish more often, and so forth. New leaders carry the world's politics now."

He reached to his side, grabbing a small tin box and handing it to Dee.

"What's this?"

"Just some reminders. We will always have Tokyo."

The limo stopped. An agent opened the door. President Freeman extended his palm to Dee. She grasped it, nodding before exiting to the same intersection they had departed from minutes before.

As the limo sped away, she opened the box. Photos and mementos greeted her. She grabbed a digital photo screen of Ko as a teenager wearing an Olympic gold medal and waving. In the photo, a younger Saburo stood at his side. An uneaten bag of souvenir peanuts from Singapore Airlines with a scribbled note that read 'I won.' An Olympic pin from the 2028 LA games. Dee removed her bullet necklace and placed it gently in the box before closing it.

"See you again someday, Ko."

***

The stray cat on the porch welcomed her with a comforting meow. A bowl of milk sat near it, partially consumed. Dee and the creature locked eyes. A calming sensation washed over her as it purred, rubbing against her leg.

Moments later, the old security door slammed as she entered her home. She placed the box and water on the table and peeled off her headphones.

"Hey, it's me. What's for breakfast?"

A voice with a southern accent responded, "Well, it ain't meat, sweetheart."

Dee turned her head as Penny emerged from the kitchen. She strolled to Dee, still in her tank top pajamas, and embraced her for a quick kiss.

"I thought we could try New York pizza," Penny said.

Dee looked at Penny's shoulder, rubbing a thumb gently over her scar.

"I've always liked pizza for breakfast. Cheese pizza," she said, emphasizing cheese.

Penny rolled her eyes. "Yes, of course, a cheese pizza. Then a show? What do you think? Time to fuel the jet?"

Dee shrugged.

"It's your money now."

Penny met her solemn tone with a finger to her lips.

"Your next words need to be more positive, okay. Only good things, remember?"

Dee expected that positivity might wear off on her someday, but for now she would play along.

"Well, if you want pizza, there are even better places than New York."

Penny thought for a moment, until her face lit up with recognition.

"Italy!" Penny screamed as she danced in circles. "Totally! Pizza with a side of seafood at the Amalfi Coast."

"Well, I'm convinced."

"Okay, shower up, stinky butt," Penny said, smacking her rear with a towel.

Dee walked away and pointed at her.

"You be careful."

"I'll make the call to fuel the Gulfstream."

***

As Dee closed the door to the bedroom, Penny's phone rang before she could dial.

"Hello?"

A tense silence permeated the line as she listened closely. No overtones. No Stingray monitoring.

"Hello?" Penny repeated.

"When is your mind like a rumpled bed?" A voice said.

Penny paused before offering a reply to the coded riddle, "When it is not made up."

"Voice identification successful. You are alone?"

"Yes. For now."

"The assets are in place. The time is now."

"It's too soon."

"You ordered readiness as soon as feasible after the Colonel's demise."

Penny grabbed the bridge of her nose.

"We're being watched. I need to get into international airspace so you can secure her for study. After her interaction with the cougar underground, it might be our most important mission."

"But do you still want to complete his mission?"

She clenched her jaw.

"Assembling that asset volume proved difficult."

"Time is short. We may not have another chance. I need your authorization as the new leader of Cell Ten."

"Yes. Do it. Proceed with the plan," Penny said. "The time has come to reveal our true capabilities to the world. If this movement is to thrive, it can't depend on my sniper skills alone. Not after I missed the shot in Tokyo."

WHAT'S NEXT?

Did you like what you read?
Leave a review!

Want more from this author? Go here.

https://bit.ly/fish-phillips-new-releases

-or-

fishphillips.com

AUTHOR INTERVIEW

What is your novel about?

Hidden Demon is an action novel about how far humanity goes to maintain the status quo for fear of change. It is a story about the only female member of the elite US Secret Service Counter Assault Team. While there is no shortage of her being a legitimate top agent, the story centers on relationships and how she processes the unique aspects of each of them as her action mission progresses. Fear. Understanding. Compassion. Humor. Anger. Revenge. She experiences them all, and it makes her a different person, ready to face the perils that come in the next phases of her story.

How did you get the idea?

This novel started as my second screenplay, which was workshopped with the Atlanta Film Society and producers in Los Angeles. Everyone who has read it can recommend no comparative work as they do not align in scope and diversity. It is a legitimate mix of high-tech science fiction, horror, technothriller, and political commentary, all steeped in real-world issues happening now and extrapolated out over twenty years.

What is the style of the novel? What can readers expect?

There are elements of Tom Clancy and Stephen King with a touch of Michael Crichton and Robin Cook, but fluff is minimal. I always write to expedite the read and get readers to the next page. I run the novel like a movie in my mind, squeezing it into three hours or fewer. I want people to enjoy the story, characters, and visuals without getting bogged down in unnecessary detail.

Epic fantasies of 100K words will never be my style, which has disappointed some readers in the past. As far as the target audience, anyone with an open mind can enjoy this story, but I think fans of political thrillers will appreciate it most, followed by science fiction and techno fans. Horror fans should also enjoy it since those components are there, but they are a smaller percentage.

The story is intense, don't expect a children's book or even a PG rating. This falls into the Adult Fiction category. There is swearing, drinking, death, and hints of sex, but you'll learn so much along the way. I don't preach in my novels. I educate. Call it the old professor in me. You might not even notice. While my stories are socially aware, I'm giving information, not telling you how to think or believe. I hope most readers appreciate an approach where I shun mindless entertainment and strive to provide the complete package. Readers should be positively glowing at the end. That is my goal.

Who is your favorite character in Hidden Demon? Who was the most difficult to write?

My favorite character this time around is Ko. He uses silence as a weapon and kicks only the rears that require it. I like his attitude. He's a gentle giant and always there for Dee, deferring to her leadership. He is the epitome of a supporting character.

The most difficult to write was Penny. She enters later in the novel. Though she presents herself as the love interest, she has many layers. Getting through them all coherently is a challenge. She is the second most complex character in the novel behind Dee.

You're a white male but you authored a book with a diverse set of characters. Any concerns about how others will receive the story?

Of course, but those concerns center around my desire to do these characters justice. They are my friends, and their diversity reflects my friends and associates in real life. This is the first time I've written a main character who is black, female, and lesbian. My supporting character is from Japan. One of the other characters is a descendant of Cuban refugees.

At the time of this interview, I am putting the book through multiple reads and asked for sensitivity reviews of both the screenplay and novel. I wanted to root out bias and problems iteratively and not let issues fester. My inevitably limited perspectives require remedy, so I treat it like a 360 evaluation in an annual performance review. What am I missing? Did I say or do anything offensive?

I can't promise to not offend anyone who picks up my book, but I have tried to write thoughtfully and respectfully from the beginning. Many of the words and actions you read are things

I've seen my real friends say or do... other than killing all those people of course.

Tell me more about the main character.

When I first started, I didn't have Dee's character profile completely fleshed out. I knew her relationship with her dad was a problem and that she hated baseball and hunting. I thought she might be from Georgia, since that's where I live right now, but I decided on Louisiana with an ancestry through the Caribbean. As characters speak, I let them author the story. I know that sounds odd, but my conversations with her, and all the characters, feed what ends up on the page. She has miles of experience as former military SpecOps and knowledge through her college education. She's vegetarian but drinks heavily and considers what's next in her mid-30's. This speaks to the dissatisfaction with her current life, which she oddly can't admit. Her reactions to Ko, her partner on the mission, and discomfort with small towns led me to ask questions. What influenced her to be this way? Why did she leave? Even though the story takes place twenty years from now, in the world I've created the perspectives in small town America have changed little.

Your last book was heavy on religious components. How does this compare?

Yes, The Last Minder had a fallen Catholic named Benny as a main character. Of course, some would say the time traveling alien was the real protagonist. I leave that to you to decide. I'm not a Catholic, so Benny required ample research. However, the Hidden Demon characters cannot be more different from him. Dee is decidedly non-religious, as is Ko. They are kindred spirits in their disdain for tradition. It is an interesting dynamic, and one reason they are both so lonely at times yet get along well together. They are walking contradictions to the world, but successful despite a measure of nonconformity. There are scenes with a church and mentions of a god, but the religious components of this book are minimal.

What makes a good story?

A presentation that helps suspend disbelief, no matter how grand the premise. Stories that draw us in and punch us in the face over and over amaze me. If I get to the end of a movie or a book after a few hours and it doesn't make me feel I'm better for the experience, then I've wasted my time. Good stories do not waste the time of others.

Do you hear from your readers much? What kinds of things do they say?

I rarely hear from readers, and if I do it is through reviews. I've never had a reader reach out directly if that's the question. I did a giveaway on Goodreads, and someone said in a review that my book had been on their "to be read" list for a long time. They were excited to win. Another said they stopped reading two other books to read mine based on the first few chapters. I am blown away by statements like that. They humble me and encourage me. Don't worry though, my wife is always there to tell me where I messed up a sentence or word choice when she reads the first drafts.

Where do you get your information or ideas for your books?

Personal experience, the Internet, magazines, news sites, interviewing others, beta readers... the list goes on. Let's just say the FBI has a profile on every writer in the world. For this book alone, I researched everything from US aircraft squadrons in Japan to artificial intelligence to torture methods to animal migration patterns. As far as ideas for books or screenplays, they simply emerge, and I capture them. That's the only way to describe it.

What is your background?

I was once interested in being a military pilot or physician or both. I completed pre-med studies at Duke University and flew multiple aircraft simulators, though I never served or went to medical school. I enjoyed technology too much. My wife and I ended up in Atlanta as we started our technology careers. After 20+ years, I'm a multi-platform creator. When I'm not writing, my software incubator for early-stage product ideas and a modest movie production company both occupy my professional time.

When did you first realize you wanted to be a writer?

When I was born. But seriously, we are all writers. I am simply privileged with the time, energy, and creative spirit to sustain it for longer than most. I'm also stubborn. So, I won't let something languish for too long. I'm all about getting it done.

Any closing thoughts?

My wife has been incredibly supportive in the journey, while my teenage daughter says, “Look at daddy signing books like he is famous.” If you want to follow me, I’m most active on Twitter, Facebook, Goodreads, Bookfunnel, and Amazon.

THANKS

As with most projects, we often turn to thanks last. A project this challenging does not happen without help.

This would have not been possible without my wife, Adeline Lake. She has stood by me during every struggle and all my successes while encouraging my creative engine. Her support makes this possible. Her gleeful use of red pens on my manuscripts improves them immensely. Having one's wife as alpha/beta reader is a blessing.

I'm grateful to my dad, MSgt John Lake (ret.), who took time from retirement to beta read and offer feedback on the military aspects of the novel on our trip to Folly Beach, SC. His participation in the process was most appreciated.

A big thank you to my developmental editor, Ilia Epifanov. Once again, he helped me find gaps in character development, story arc and world building. His questions and insights enriched the chapter beats, so I could tell this story to its fullest.

A special thanks to Karen Holcomb Gonzalez. As a long-time professional acquaintance and friend, she has taken an active interest in both my fiction and non-fiction work. She is also the biggest Star Trek fan I know. Her beta read of the novel offered valuable feedback from the consumer perspective.

Thank you to Julie Hurwitz who took the time to review the screenplay version of this story and provide feedback prior to conversion to a novel. As a writer, set designer, and UX professional I was appreciative for her time.

Thanks to my old high school friend, Ruth Shiroma Foster, for reviewing parts of the screenplay dialogue early on. To Miho Moore who provided feedback on the proper use of kanji characters. Thanks to Casey Barbato Case for the great thrift shop name. A brief but gracious thanks to Roxanne Hiatt, who has supplied substantial insight on fiction marketing. I deeply appreciate her help.

CPSIA information can be obtained
at www.ICGtesting.com
Printed in the USA
FSHW022109250821
83992FS